'What **[...]** ng?'

'At the moment, none.'

Before the meeting disbanded, Heather noticed that the staff had acceptance written across their features. Aaron Spence had done an excellent job of convincing them that they wouldn't experience any major upheavals for the time being.

Unfortunately, she didn't fall into the same category. His mere presence had shaken her world in earthquake proportions.

Jessica Matthews' interest in medicine began at a young age and she nourished it with medical stories and hospital-based television programmes. After a stint as a teenage candy striper, she pursued a career as a clinical laboratory scientist. When not writing or on duty, she fills her day with countless family- and school-related activities. Jessica lives in the central US with her husband, daughter and son.

THE CALL OF DUTY

BY

JESSICA MATTHEWS

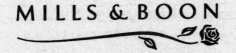

MILLS & BOON

To Renee Roszel and Leslie LaFoy, for your
unfailing encouragement and advice.

MILLS & BOON, the Rose Device and LOVE ON CALL
are trademarks of the publisher.
Harlequin Mills & Boon Limited,
Eton House, 18–24 Paradise Road, Richmond, Surrey TW9 1SR
This edition published by arrangement with
Harlequin Enterprises B.V.

© Jessica Matthews 1995

ISBN 0 263 79337 0

Set in 10 on 12 pt Linotron Times
03-9509-50150

Typeset in Great Britain by CentraCet, Cambridge
Made and printed in Great Britain

CHAPTER ONE

'I DID everything I possibly could.' With a white-knuckled grip on the telephone receiver, Heather Manning clenched her jaw until it ached and twisted the flexible cord into one more knot.

'Obviously you did something the selection committee wasn't happy with,' Richard Manning the Third retorted. 'Otherwise they'd have promoted you instead of bringing in some outsider.'

'I've worked to the best of my ability, Dad. You can't expect me to do more than that.'

'Hmmph! You've disappointed me, Heather. I really thought you'd go places, but I was sadly mistaken. You don't have the drive a physician needs to succeed.'

She drew a shaky breath. She felt badly enough over the news she'd received thirty minutes ago; she didn't need her father's diatribe too. 'I have to go now. Someone's waiting to see me.' The white lie gave her the control she needed to stop his harangue.

'I'll call again in a few days.'

Wonderful, she thought, cradling the receiver. Thank goodness that was over! With reverent fingertips, she traced the polished edge of the oak desk she'd come to regard as her own. The abrupt and unexpected turn her life had taken still seemed unbelievable. The chief of pathology position had been yanked from what she had considered a relatively secure grasp.

She frowned. The concept of rewarding work well

done was a myth—a legend perpetuated by authoritarians who thrived on their power. In her case, the man dangling the proverbial carrot had been Paul Carter.

When Dr Carter, Plainview Medical Center's chief of staff, and Judith Dalton, hospital administrator, had invited her to lunch at the finest establishment in town, Heather had been delighted to accept. It was no secret among the staff that Dr Carter preferred to combine business with pleasure and more than one physician had been promoted or at least honored over the dinner table. Her noon appointment, she'd been reasonably certain, meant Dr Carter intended to change her own title from acting chief to chief.

But as the meal had progressed and they'd discussed every topic imaginable except the one dearest to her heart her excitement had slowly transformed into fear—fear that this special luncheon had become a consolation prize rather than an occasion to celebrate.

And it had.

Heather swallowed, but the burning lump in her throat refused to disappear. She looked around the office she'd used for the last six months—longer if the truth were known—and felt the same searing sensation develop behind her eyes.

Even though it was Friday afternoon and most employees had gone home, she refused to express her disappointment in a more traditional manner. A female professional seen with tears streaming down her face would only make her colleagues agree that she didn't possess the character strength to assume command of a busy, stressful department.

With anger finally surfacing above gut-wrenching disappointment, she crossed the room to retrieve an empty cardboard box—the one she'd confiscated from the pile destined for Plainview Medical Center's incinerator. Retracing her steps, her barely audible footfalls seemed eerie in the room where classical or rock-and-roll music usually played in the background. She dropped the container on to the plush executive chair.

After a few clumsy yanks to separate the top desk drawer from its roller tracks, she upended it over the carton. Meticulously arranged paper clips, pens, a few tubes of lipstick and other assorted necessities rumbled like an avalanche as they landed in a heap. At this point, neatness counted for nothing. The sooner she cleared the room of her presence the better, she told herself grimly.

She repositioned the drawer, slammed it closed, then repeated the process with another.

'When did you get back? I've been so anxious to hear how your lunch went.' Kim Whitfield, Heather's friend and only employee trained as a cytotechnologist to examine cells microscopically, spoke from the doorway. She sounded excited and her face held an expectant expression.

'I've had more enjoyable meals.' Heather's words came out crisp as she thumbed through a pile of seminar leaflets before tossing them in the trash. The cuisine had lived up to the restaurant's five-star reputation, but by the time the waiter had served the chocolate mousse she'd lost her appetite. She wondered how long it would take to dissociate Chez Robert's specialty from a desperate, sinking feeling in the pit of her stomach.

'Oh, no. You didn't hear good news.' Kim's freckled face wrinkled with worry as she walked up to the desk.

Heather pitched a folder into the metal can with the

ease of a basketball star. 'Whatever gave you that idea?' she retorted, wincing at her uncharacteristic cynicism. She knelt on the floor to rummage through the lower drawers. Her tawny collar-length hair fell into her face and she tucked the errant locks behind her ears before continuing her quest for more personal belongings. Seconds later, several pocket reference guides, a hand-held calculator and a spare box of tissues noisily joined her other possessions in the half-full box.

She rose and surveyed the desk, her hands on her hips. With her personal effects gone and only a few generic office supplies remaining, the drawers looked barren.

'Oh, Heather. I'm so sorry,' Kim commiserated.

'Oh, good, you're back, Dr Manning. When do we get to cele——?' Emily Tate, Heather's fun-loving and often forgetful secretary, stopped mid-sentence when she saw the grim expressions on the two women's faces.

'Anytime you'd like.' Pleased that her voice sounded so normal despite the frustration and disappointment still eating a hole in the back of her throat, Heather continued. 'The selection committee finally chose our new chief pathologist. Dr Aaron Spence will be taking over those duties effective Monday morning at eight o'clock. With all this free time, I can follow your advice to relax and enjoy myself.'

'What did Dr Carter and Judith Dalton say? Did they explain their obviously idiotic decision?' Kim asked, indignation dripping off every word.

Pausing from her task, Heather fingered the small locket hanging below her neckline. She popped it open and closed, then ran it back and forth along a few inches of gold chain while she recalled the lunchtime conversation. When Dr Carter had addressed her using a tone of gentle sympathy, she'd known the committee hadn't decided in her favor.

'Heather,' Paul Carter, chief of staff, had begun after the cappuccino had been poured. 'We appreciate and recognize your efforts during the five years you've been with us, especially since Dr Walker had his heart attack six months ago.'

But. . .she had sensed he'd say next, and he had.

'But we felt we needed a more seasoned individual, one with more experience, to take over Dr Walker's position. Please don't misunderstand,' he'd quickly added. 'With your credentials and the excellent job you've done in very trying circumstances, we didn't arrive at our decision easily.'

Dr Carter had finished with a gentle admonition. 'I'm sure that you'll work with Dr Spence as well as you did with Dr Walker and I know our newest physician will appreciate your efforts to make his transition into leadership a smooth one.'

The chain snapped, releasing the oval pendant into Heather's hand. She stared at it numbly, wondering how many necklaces she'd destroy during the next few weeks. During times of personal stress—and today had all the earmarks of being one of those periods—her jewelry bore the brunt of her inner turmoil.

Knowing that Kim and Emily were waiting for her reply, she dropped the pieces into her pocket, and pretended a nonchalance she didn't feel. 'Dr Carter said the selection committee had decided to hire some-one with more experience.'

Kim threw her hands in the air to emphasize her outrage. 'Experience? What do they think you've been doing all this time? Holding down a chair and filing your fingernails? And what about all those times Dr Carter said you were doing an excellent job?'

Heather shrugged. She'd posed that very question. The chief of staff's answer had been as evasive as his eye contact. Judith Dalton, however, had been quick to point out that Plainview Medical simply *couldn't* let an applicant with such an excellent background slip through its fingers. Recalling the svelte brunette's drawl and patronizing tone of voice, she grimaced in disgust.

'I know what it is,' Emily added, nodding her frizzy, perm-damaged head for emphasis. 'They think thirty-one is too young, especially with your slender figure and beautiful brown eyes. You might get married and leave them in the lurch. I still think you should wear higher-heeled shoes. It's hard for these males to consider you as an authority figure when they're always looking down at you.' She paused, studying her superior. 'I wish you'd let me color your hair. You know how blondes are stereotyped.'

'Sorry, Em, but my low pumps are fine, I like my natural hair color, and if I look too young time will take care of that,' Heather remarked.

Emily frowned. 'It's just too bad your parents didn't give you a no-nonsense name like Margaret or Catherine.'

A long-forgotten memory came to Heather's mind and her ache lessened. Her mother had insisted on that name after conceiving her daughter during a trip to Scotland. As a child, Heather had never tired of hearing that story.

'When did you say this Dr Spence starts?' Kim asked.

'Monday.'

'But today is Friday,' Kim protested. 'That's not very much notice.'

'No, it isn't.' Heather had her own theories about the sly tactics but didn't want to plant them in her loyal staff's heads. Dr Spence's reasoning might have been a simple matter of avoiding the usual fanfare made over new medical personnel, but deep down she suspected that he simply didn't want to give her an opportunity to resign before he reported for duty.

'What will you do?' Kim's eyes grew wide.

'I'm going to finish cleaning off my. . .this desk, and then get ready for Monday's surgeries.' Heather thumbed through papers, well aware that Kim wasn't asking for her immediate plans. The cytotech, as well as a few other close friends, knew she had worked hard in preparation for the day she'd claim the title of chief pathologist. Today's news had just squelched her prospects at this hospital.

Heather scooped the loose pages of notes for her upcoming pathology presentation on liver disease into a haphazard pile. As she crammed them into the box, her mind raced off at several different tangents.

Yes, she'd bet her diploma that the last-minute announcement was intended to prevent her from leaving Plainview before Dr Walker's replacement arrived. Tempting though it was, she couldn't walk out without giving the required thirty-day notice. Even if she didn't object to the loss of a glowing reference and the permanent blot on her record, her sense of fair play wouldn't allow her to resort to such shoddy, immature tactics. But she *would* study her professional journals' classified ads, update her curriculum vitae, and begin sending out query letters as early as next week. With luck and perseverance, she'd be gone in a matter of months. After all, she had her own career goals to pursue.

On that positive note, she gathered an armful of files from the cabinet and handed them to Emily.

'This is an absolute injustice,' Emily declared, her green eyes flashing. 'You took over a lot of Dr Walker's duties even before his heart attack. You covered for him so many times when he wasn't——'

'Life isn't fair and it's foolish to expect it to be,' Heather interrupted, repeating what she'd told herself many times during the past hour. 'I did what I had to do and I don't have any regrets. I'm just sorry that the medical community lost a fine man.'

'You're certainly taking this well.' Emily's eyes held awe as she studied the young pathologist. 'I'd be screaming my head off.'

Heather clenched her hands into fists. If they only knew how close she was to doing that very thing. . . Having a dream snatched away that was once within reach wasn't easy to accept.

'Do you know anything about this Dr Spence?' Kim asked.

Heather took a deep breath, grateful that the questioning had turned away from her personal feelings. 'I think he's from Maryland. He's spent a number of years in the military, worked at several veterans' administration hospitals and co-authored several pathology textbooks.' She knew her two dinner companions had praised the man's accomplishments, but she'd been so caught up with keeping her emotions under control that she only recalled bits and pieces of the man's résumé. To be honest, she couldn't have cared less if he'd been the President's personal physician.

'Hmmph!' Emily's disgust was evident.

'If he plans to run things like a military operation, there'll be a lot of unhappy cowboys at this ranch,' Kim threatened, slipping into her husband's country western vernacular.

'Maybe you'll be lucky and he'll be close to retirement age,' Emily mentioned.

'He has a lot of experience but I doubt he's that old, Em. I'd say he'll be around for another ten or fifteen years—a lot longer than I will, I'm sure.' Heather stacked her reference books on one corner of the desk instead of replacing them on the wall-to-wall bookshelf. 'Whatever you may feel, keep in mind that Dr Carter has eyes everywhere. I've already been politely warned that he expects Dr Spence to enjoy a smooth transition into his new duties.'

Amid choruses of 'of course' and 'most definitely', Heather studied the seemingly innocent faces of her two associates. 'You're thinking something. And I can tell it isn't pretty.' The smirks on Emily's and Kim's faces coaxed her mouth into a slight curve.

'I'd be happy to help Dr Spence find his way around the lab,' Kim volunteered. 'There are all kinds of pitfalls an unsuspecting person could stumble across. By the way, did I ever tell you that my oldest son rigged the safety shower in his chemistry class to spray water whenever someone walked underneath it?'

Heather's smile reached her eyes as she envisioned a gray-headed Aaron Spence with water dripping down his suit on to his spit-polished shoes. Her spirits lifted.

'And I can put black shoe paste on the microscope eyepieces,' Kim added, her brown eyes gleaming and her carroty curls bouncing with undisguised enjoyment. 'After he reads slides, he'll look like a racoon.'

Heather entertained another unflattering picture of her new superior, and this time she couldn't hold back a chuckle. 'You wouldn't dare.'

'And I can try out some ideas from this new herb book I bought,' Emily added. 'There's something I can put in his coffee that will make sure he becomes very familiar with the men's room. Now let me think what it is.' She closed her eyes and tapped her forehead.

'Cascara,' answered a deep voice from the doorway.

'I beg your pardon?' Heather glanced at the man poised on the threshold carrying a leather briefcase. Her initial impression tallied with a clichéd description of tall, dark and handsome, although she added 'serious' to the list.

'The herb you're wanting to use is cascara buckthorn. I thought you might like to know.'

Heather wondered what else the man had overheard. 'Is there something we can help you with?'

'I hope so. Although I'd love to continue our discussion on medicinal plants, I'm looking for Dr Manning. Heather Manning.'

'I'm Dr Manning.'

He raised his eyebrows as if he didn't believe her.

Refusing to flinch under the man's impertinent stare, she straightened her shoulders, knowing her action added very little height to her five-foot-four-inch frame.

She matched the visitor's analytical perusal with one of her own. His thick walnut-brown hair had a faint glimmer of silver at the temples. Equally dark eyebrows arched above slate-colored eyes, giving him a cool, brooding air. A squared jaw, defined cheekbones and a straight nose completed the picture. His features, combined with a self-assured stance, probably drew second and even third glances from young and old females alike.

It was evident that the navy blue polo shirt covered broad shoulders and the tan cotton twill trousers clothed a muscle-toned body at least eight inches taller than her own. She wondered whether he might be the sales representative she'd been expecting, but doubted it. In her experience, a company man looking for business wore a suit and tie as standard attire.

'I'm Aaron Spence.'

This was Aaron Spence? This striking fellow who couldn't be much over forty? Heather clenched her teeth together to keep her jaw from dropping open. Inwardly she groaned, wondering what other surprises the day still held.

'Er, Dr Spence. This is my—er—our secretary, Emily Tate, and our cytotech, Kim Whitfield,' Heather pointed out, rapidly composing herself.

'We were just helping Dr Manning,' Emily fluttered, clutching the files to her chest and looking to her companions for reassurance.

'I'm sure,' Dr Spence replied.

His cynical note wasn't wasted on the flabbergasted trio. 'We'll just take these .things to your office, Heath—Dr Manning.' Kim grabbed the pile of reference books before exiting on Emily's heels.

'I understood you wouldn't be here until Monday,' Heather began, thrusting her hands deep into her pockets.

'Officially, yes. But I wanted to get settled so I'd be ready to step into your routine.'

'Of course.' She grabbed her favorite coffee cup off a bookshelf and stuffed it into her box.

'I am in the right room, aren't I? The sign above the door says chief of pathology.'

'Yes, you are. I'll have my things out of here in a minute.'

'I didn't realize this was your office.'

'It isn't.'

He quirked one eyebrow and she hastened to explain. 'It was Dr Walker's, but it was easier for me to take over in here.'

'I see.'

Somehow she was afraid that he didn't. She sensed that he suspected her to be a grasping, power-hungry female, but she doubted an explanation would change his opinion. Fate must be laughing that the man who could make her employment either enjoyable or a living hell had arrived before she'd removed all traces of her occupancy.

Kim reappeared and Heather thrust the box into her subordinate's hands. As she pivoted round, Heather's glance fell on the corner where a pot of Swedish ivy hung above a diffenbachia planter. Indecision plagued her. Should she leave them for him to appreciate, or run the risk of appearing juvenile by removing them?

'Nice plants,' he mentioned, as though reading her thoughts. He placed his briefcase on the desk and removed several picture frames.

'They get plenty of sun in here.' Accepting the fact that they wouldn't live long in her cubicle because of limited natural light, she decided to maintain the status quo—at least as long as the room's occupant cared for them properly. And if the plants stayed, her handmade hummingbird suncatcher might as well too.

A quick glance around the office told her she'd left

nothing else behind. 'We keep our reference books in here for lack of other space, but if you find a few volumes missing I have them.'

'No problem.'

'If you need anything, we'll be a few doors down the hall.'

'Plotting more nefarious activities?' His face was inscrutable. Immediately she knew he'd overheard the bulk of their conversation. If anything out of the ordinary occurred in the days to come, she knew that she and her two cohorts would be at the top of his suspect list.

'No. We were just. . .just letting off steam. The girls didn't mean anything by it.'

'No doubt.'

His dry tone sent her to the door. 'Well, if you'll excuse me. . .'

After his brief nod, she fled into her sanctuary and the company of friends.

'He's nothing like Dr Walker, is he?' Kim remarked in a low voice. Emily seconded her opinion with a vehement nod.

'It appears not.' Heather shook her head, comparing Noah's easygoing manner with the formality of his successor. In the space of a few minutes, Aaron Spence had made her feel as if *she* were the new kid—the rookie—reporting for duty instead of the other way around. No doubt she sounded as stiff as she felt. She hadn't suffered the usual new job jitters under Noah's direction and hated to think that she now had to please such a stern taskmaster.

'Do you need some help tidying up?' Kim asked.

Heather glanced around the small area already filled

to capacity with only her desk and two filing cabinets. Although she didn't consider herself claustrophobic, the office would be unbearable if she didn't have the evergreen-blocked window to give a small illusion of space. 'Thanks, but I'll manage.' Even if there had been room for two people to work, she needed time alone to put her thoughts in order.

Kim nodded and disappeared while Heather popped a cassette tape into her player. Lively strains of Beethoven's 'Turkish March' filled the air.

She once again perused the mess and half-heartedly attempted to bring order to the chaos. Lack of storage space posed the greatest problem and she found herself doing nothing more than making neat piles on top of the filing cabinets. By the time Kim and the lab tech knocked on her open door, she'd done all she could.

'Melody found an unusual slide and she brought it to me. I thought you'd better take a look at it.' Kim handed the purple-stained blood film over to Heather.

'What do we have?' she asked, whipping the cover off her microscope.

Melody spoke up while the pathologist scanned the specimen. 'It's from a four-year-old girl, Caitlin Burns. According to Dr Wheeler's nurse, Mrs Burns stated that Caitlin hadn't been ill, but she became concerned when she discovered large patches of dark red, pin-point-sized spots all over her body.'

From the description, Heather pictured tiny capillaries bleeding into the skin and understood Mrs Burns' fright. 'What was Jim Wheeler's opinion?'

Melody shrugged. 'I think he's expecting our report to give him the answers.'

Heather adjusted the focus knob. 'Children this age

normally have a lot of lymphocytes because those cells are responsible for building their immunity. But everyone needs a certain percentage of the cells that fight bacterial infections. Unfortunately, that's where Caitlin is horribly deficient. Has she had a complete blood count before?'

Melody shook her head. 'This is her first CBC.'

'Well, she could be suffering from either a low-grade viral infection or something much worse, like lymphocytic leukemia. Thanks for bringing this to my attention,' Heather said, drawing the telephone closer.

When the pediatrician answered, she began without preamble. 'I've reviewed a blood smear on one of your patients, Jim. Caitlin Burns. Her total white blood cell count is depressed and we've found one hundred per cent lymphs. By any chance, has she been vaccinated recently?'

'No. Any other ideas?'

She voiced the same opinions she'd given Kim and Melody, finishing with, 'I'd keep a close eye on her, Jim. If her abnormal blood picture is due to a viral infection, it should revert to normal in a few weeks. If it doesn't, I'd have to recommend an oncology consult and/or a bone marrow. It probably wouldn't hurt to rule out any clotting disorders.'

He agreed and Heather experienced a satisfied feeling that little Caitlin would be closely monitored. Hopefully her condition was only an aftereffect of a lingering virus and not something much, much worse. . .

Once she'd documented her recommendations and mentioned to Melody that she'd like to see the child on her next visit, she headed for the histology lab where tissue samples were examined. Mondays were hectic enough without having the added stress of a new boss looking over everyone's shoulder. Kim and the other technicians were usually prepared, but it wouldn't hurt to double-check.

She smiled when she saw Kim cleaning the dual-head teaching microscope. 'I thought you'd already done that once today?'

Kim grinned, liberally spraying the eyepieces with canned air to dry them. 'My mother always said, "Kim, cleanliness is next to godliness," and after meeting Dr Spence I don't want to take any chances that he'll find fault with the way we take care of our equipment.'

'Good idea.' Heather glanced around the room and found everything in order.

'The surgery schedule is on the counter. I'll post it before I leave.'

Heather studied the typed page. 'Doesn't look too bad for a Monday—a hip pinning, a hysterectomy, and the usual breast biopsies. The bowel obstruction could prove interesting if the surgeon has to remove part of the colon. But overall the cases look fairly routine.'

'By the way,' Kim mentioned as she tucked the microscope under its dust cover, 'Dr Osborne called about a bone marrow on Martin Jenner. He said you had all the details, so I scheduled him for Tuesday.'

'Good.'

Hesitating on the threshold, Aaron Spence took advantage of the women's inattention to study his newest colleague. Dr Carter's description hadn't done Dr Manning justice and her petite youthfulness had come as a complete surprise when he'd met her an hour ago. He'd spent the time since then reading personnel files, admitting to himself that the special attention he paid to Dr Manning's records appeased his masculine curiosity as well as his professional interest.

He'd recognized the schools she'd attended as the exclusive, private institutions they were. But her high marks and academic honors seemed inconsistent with Dr Carter's thinly veiled suggestions that the department needed guidance and strong supervision now that Dr Walker wasn't on the scene. He knew of several physicians who were exceptional scholars but mediocre in practical application and he intended to discover if Dr Manning fell into the same category. If so, he wouldn't hesitate to comply with Dr Carter's directive to clean out the proverbial deadwood.

'What's the scoop on the tonsillectomy case?' he heard Kim ask.

'Chronic throat infections. His lab work is within normal limits for a five-year-old and the surgeon isn't anticipating any excessive bleeding problems,' Heather replied.

Aaron found himself enjoying the melodious quality of Heather's voice and couldn't believe that an attractive woman like her had never married. He wondered if she fell into the single-but-looking-for-marriage category, or if she was an avowed professional who lived only for her job. If it was the latter, he might run into some resistance as he took over the department.

He rubbed his right knee, shifting his weight slightly on to his left leg to lessen the ache. The pain was worse today than usual, probably because of the days he'd spent driving to reach Plainview. It was no wonder the practical jokes he'd overheard hadn't seemed humorous at the time, although in the past he'd instigated a few harmless pranks of his own.

He drew a quiet breath. What a nasty quirk of fate that the first woman he'd found interesting in a long time was a surbordinate. Office romances usually didn't work well in the long run and if he had to fire her or one of her friends he'd be in the middle of an extremely messy situation.

'Dr Spence. I didn't hear you. We were just going over Monday's surgery list,' Heather reported, thankful that they'd been talking shop. His relaxed stance and folded arms indicated that he'd been waiting there for some time.

'So I hear. Anything interesting?'

His approach sent shivers rippling down her spine and she attributed them to nervousness rather than excitement. 'Nothing out of the ordinary.'

'I see.'

'I hate to run, but. . .' Kim interjected, scooting toward the door.

'Have a nice weekend,' Heather called, wishing she could follow her friend but knowing she couldn't. Turning to Dr Spence, she asked, 'Would you like to see the lab now, or would you rather wait?'

'I'll wait, but I do have one question, Dr Manning.'

She waited expectantly. Intent on his face, his blue eyes in particular, she barely noticed him thrust one hand into his coat pocket. Her face froze at the sight of the familiar article he'd retrieved.

'Are these yours?'

Dangling from his fingers was a pair of pantyhose.

CHAPTER TWO

HEATHER stared in horror at the intimate apparel she'd forgotten she'd stashed in the closet for an emergency. Feeling hot blood course through her cheeks, she stifled the impulse to grab the hosiery out of his hand. Slowly, she extended her arm. Warm fingertips settled against her palm, making her dimly aware of rough hands and calluses. Calluses? Grateful that her superior hadn't discovered any items more personal than a pair of nylons—it could have been much worse—she stuffed them into her lab coat pocket and murmured her thanks.

'You're welcome.'

She thought she heard amusement in Dr Spence's voice and a glance confirmed her opinion. His mouth had curved into a soft smile and his eyes seemed a warmer shade of blue. Goodness! When the man smiled he appeared even more handsome than she'd first thought.

'I'd say we're even. Wouldn't you?'

His humor somehow relieved the tension she'd felt since she'd met him. He obviously didn't hold any grudges, but just to make sure. . . 'Emily and Kim really didn't mean anything personal,' she began.

'I know. They're afraid I'll turn the lab into a military operation. Don't worry, I won't.'

'They'll be glad to hear that.' She knew that if he'd overheard more of their conversation he would have known the exact cause of her friends' righteous anger. Since it wouldn't serve any useful purpose to announce that he'd received the position that most people—herself included—had thought would be hers, she let the subject drop. Someday, if circumstances warranted it, she might correct his erroneous conclusion.

'I think I'll call it a day,' Aaron remarked, shifting his weight again. 'I have more unpacking to do and I doubt my son accomplished a lot in my absence.'

'Son?' Before she could stop herself, Heather looked down at his left hand. His ring finger was bare and completely tanned.

'Joshua is twelve—teetering on the brink of becoming a teenager.'

'Ah. Old enough to know better and too young to do the fun stuff.'

'You sound familiar with that age group.'

She nodded. 'I have friends with kids in middle school so I've been exposed to their idiosyncrasies. Do you have any other children?'

'No. My wife died a number of years ago. Car accident.'

'I'm sorry,' Heather murmured.

He acknowledged her condolences with a nod and reached in his back pocket for his well-worn billfold. 'If you need help this weekend, feel free to call me.' After jotting several numbers across the face of a business card, he passed it to her and turned to leave.

She noticed his limp. 'Are you all right?'

He swung round, his dark eyebrows lifted and his blue eyes questioning. She pointed. 'Your leg.'

He grinned. 'A remnant of my careless youth.'

'Football?'

'Softball,' he corrected her. 'It usually doesn't bother me, but when it does. . .' he shrugged '. . .my son tells me I lose my sense of humor.'

Heather sensed his explanation was meant to be an apology, even if it had been delivered in a roundabout manner. She felt that their future working relationship hinged on how she accepted his olive branch.

'I'll keep that in mind,' she said lightly. 'But should you be lifting and carrying?'

'Probably not. But since I don't want to live out of a suitcase for weeks on end I have no choice. Are you by any chance volunteering your services, Dr Manning?'

She chewed on her bottom lip, unable to say yes and unwilling to say no. 'I wouldn't be much help anyway.'

'Bad back?'

'Lousy muscles.'

Aaron smiled. 'Luckily the movers are responsible for the heavy things and Josh and I can manage the rest.'

He gave her a casual farewell salute and she watched him leave. Strangely enough, his absence made the room seem cold and empty. How ridiculous, she thought as she flicked off the lights.

She arrived home ten minutes later to find a blinking light on her answering machine.

'Heather, this is your father. Have you heard about your promotion yet? Call me.'

Richard Manning's forceful voice hung in the air as the tape whirred. At least she wouldn't have to return his call since he, impatient as usual, had already phoned her at the hospital. Feeling a familiar ache build, she rubbed her midsection. After years of hearing her father's censure, even a high-tech copy of his familiar tone sent her acid production into high gear.

She chewed two chalky-tasting tablets guaranteed to relieve her symptoms, poured a glass of low-fat milk and settled on to the couch next to a stack of recent pathology journals. The first one had two positions available that appeared interesting and she marked those. But even as she scanned the ads questions bobbed to the surface like corks on water. Was searching for a new job the right thing to do? Was she being too hasty?

Dismay flooded into the pit of her stomach at the thought of leaving Plainview. She'd lived in the community for over five years and had developed a circle of good friends. In addition, she'd finally decorated her home to her taste. Why did *she* have to start over?

Heather closed her eyes and a picture of Dr Spence appeared. Of all the men she'd met and worked with over the years, why did she have to find herself attracted to her boss? Even if situations such as these ended well—and they usually didn't—she'd never reach her goal to become head of a department.

And that meant too much to her and her father to give it up now.

Early Monday morning, Heather strode into a semi-private room on the surgical unit. Approaching the silver-haired woman sitting in the first bed, she introduced herself.

'Oh, yes,' Matilda Hill replied. 'My doctor said you'd be in to see me.'

Heather took up a position near the foot of the bed. 'As Dr Franklin has probably explained, after the surgeon removes a portion of the lump in your breast, he'll send it to me in the lab and I'll do what's called a frozen section. It's a quick process that allows us to look at the cells microscopically and determine if the tumor is malignant. The surgeon will know within a few minutes what he's dealing with and then take appropriate action.'

'A mastectomy, right?' Mrs Hill's dark eyes looked to Heather's for confirmation.

'It's possible. But nothing will be done until I determine what type of cell is causing the growth. Not all breast tumors are malignant, you know.'

The woman eyed her cautiously. 'So everything hinges on your report. You look awfully young to know your business. What if you make a mistake?'

'It's my job *not* to make a mistake.'

The elderly lady crossed her arms over a well-endowed chest and harrumphed. 'That's what they all say. What if it's something you've never seen before? I declare doctors are getting younger all the time.'

Heather smiled at the familiar complaint made by senior citizens. 'In the unlikely event that your case is unusual, I'll confer with our other pathologist. If both of us are stymied, we'll send your tissue sample to the Mayo Clinic in Minnesota. Don't worry, we'll take good care of you.

'Aren't these beautiful flowers?' she offered, deliberately changing the subject. Mrs Hill smiled and began a lengthy discussion on the thoughtfulness of her grandchildren. By the time Heather excused herself, the patient's lined face was visibly relaxed. Even though she was now behind schedule, Heather considered the extra time she'd spent with the elderly woman well worth the effort.

Her happiness plummeted, however, when she arrived in the tissue lab.

'Dr Spence has been waiting for you and let me tell you he isn't a patient man,' Kim remarked in a low voice. 'He's with Emily now.'

Heather sighed. She didn't seem too successful at making a favorable impression. Maybe he'd be more understanding after she explained her tardiness. She'd just reached the doorway when he looked up from his file of reports.

'Heather,' he acknowledged, simultaneously rising and dropping the folder on the desk.

'Good morning, Aaron. Emily.' Taking his lead, she didn't use his professional title. She'd always been on a first-name basis with her colleagues and was relieved that he'd chosen to do the same. Heather stepped aside and followed him out of the nervous secretary's office.

Seeing him clad in the dark blue, baggy, hospital-issue surgical scrubs made her realize that the man radiated an aura of power no matter what he wore. His tunic's vee-neckline exposed curly dark hair that she found oddly unsettling.

He was as handsome as she'd remembered.

'I'm sorry I wasn't here when you arrived this morning, but I had a patient to see.'

'Oh, really?'

His questioning look prompted her to explain. 'At Dr Janet Franklin's request, I started visiting with her breast biopsy patients prior to surgery. There was such a positive response, several others asked if I'd call on their patients too. Of course, I only drop in where I have the personal physician's approval.'

Heather decided not to name those few, but powerful men who thought she overstepped her bounds by doing so, nor did she care to explain why this project was so dear to her own heart.

'How much time does this take out of your day?'

'Not that much. Maybe one or two hours a week, depending on the number of cases. The hospital's patient care surveys show that our clients are very appreciative and so, in the interest of public relations, I don't think we should stop——'

He held up one hand. 'You don't have to sell me on the idea, Heather. If the patients are happy and the doctors are cooperative, we'll continue with your program. But if something changes. . .' He shrugged.

Encouraged by this small victory, she wanted to shout for joy. Perhaps he'd also accept some of her other ideas, ideas she'd been unable to implement because of resistance from the chief of staff. Succumbing to her lighthearted mood, she asked, 'Did you have a good weekend?'

'If you mean did I accomplish a lot, yes, I did. If you're asking if Josh and I had fun, no, we didn't.'

'Maybe next weekend you will. Have fun, that is.'

'I hope so. You mentioned you knew kids Josh's age. Do you think we could get them together so he'll have some time to get to know them before school starts?'

'No problem. I'll see what I can arrange.'

'By the way,' he asked, 'is Emily always so disorganized? Her filing system is a disaster. I can't help but think she's not suited to secretarial work.'

'Emily does all right, although I must admit she has

an unorthodox method of keeping records. She's a person who gives new meaning to the label "a creature of habit" and we've learned to honor her quirks. It keeps her from becoming flustered.' She made a mental note to pay close attention to the reports she'd sign over the next the few days, at least until the secretary got used to her new boss.

'Have you met everyone yet?' she asked, hurrying to match his long strides.

'Kim took care of the introductions since you weren't here.'

Although he spoke without rancor, she sensed his displeasure. She really should have been there to welcome him to the department but her visit with Mrs Hill had taken longer than she'd expected. Hopefully her staff wouldn't interpret her tardiness as a passive-aggressive response to the new boss. If so, she'd have to rectify the situation.

One more step brought them into the histology lab where the first batch of morning tissue samples lined the counter. Realizing that her small-sized disposable gloves wouldn't fit Aaron's extra-large-sized hands, she stood on tiptoe to reach in a cabinet. 'We stashed this box away since no one could wear them. But I think they'll fit you.'

Aaron tugged a pair on to his hands with a snap. Wiggling his gloved fingers, he said, 'Perfect.'

Both of them were examining a section of colon when the intercom buzzed and a faceless voice reported, 'Dr Manning? Mrs Hill is on her way into OR. Room two.'

'Thank you,' she called out, stripping off the used gloves to wash her hands. Aaron accompanied her to a door a few feet away.

'We do our frozen sections in here, but I'm trying to set up an area in the surgery suite for us.' She crossed the threshold of another room and sat in front of the chamber where the tissue was frozen, then sliced into nearly transparent sections. As he joined her, she suddenly became conscious of the tight quarters. On occasion she'd shared the cramped conditions of the oversized closet with a visiting pathology resident, but for some strange reason it hadn't seemed as tiny. She fiddled unnecessarily with the dials, noticing how the close confines made his masculine scent more potent.

It certainly is warm in here today, she thought, tempted to wipe away the perspiration she felt on her brow. Though she hated to admit it, nervousness rather than the ambient temperature was the cause of her schoolgirl reaction.

A few minutes later, to her relief, a floating nurse carried in a small stainless-steel kidney basin. As predicted, only a short time elapsed before Heather made her diagnosis. Benign. Mrs Hill, like any woman facing a possible mastectomy, would be pleased by the good news.

She quickly punched OR's code into the intercom and reported her findings to the surgeon, Dave Franklin.

'Thanks, Heather. After I saw it I suspected as much,' he called out. 'Hey, Janet tells me you have some new help down there.'

'Yes, I do. As a matter of fact, Dr Spence is with me right now.' She prayed Dave would take the subtle warning and refrain from further comment.

'Call us when you have some free time and we'll

throw a party,' he mentioned. 'Sponge,' she heard him request.

'Will do. See you later.' She flipped the intercom switch to 'OFF', pleased that the conversation hadn't included 'congratulations on your new job', although when Dave had mentioned throwing a party she'd crossed her fingers. The Franklins were her closest friends and the couple knew how much she'd wanted and worked for the promotion. They'd been out of town the past weekend and, because of the busy Monday schedules, Heather hadn't told them the latest news yet. But it didn't matter; they'd find out before the day ended, courtesy of the infamous hospital grapevine. Hopefully, Aaron would interpret Dave's party remark in a neutral way, thinking that they simply wanted to celebrate the arrival of another pathologist to share the burden.

'How long ago did you say Walker died? Six months?' Aaron broke the lull in conversation during their return to the lab.

She blinked, startled out of her preoccupation. 'Yes—give or take a few weeks.'

'Since you've worked alone since then, I realize you've dealt with everything that came in. What was your routine when you had another pathologist?'

Heather bit her lip. In the beginning, they had established a workable system, but circumstances had quickly altered their plans. Should she admit that she'd gradually taken on more duties until it reached the point where she had shouldered the majority of the load?

'It varied, depending on Noah's schedule,' she prevaricated. 'We tried to divide the work—one of us prepared the tissue sections and performed autopsies while the other read the abnormal pap smears and handled the other microscopic exams. Each week we'd switch jobs.'

He nodded and she wasn't certain if he approved of the idea or simply acknowledged that that was the way they'd run things. His gaze was focused down the corridor when he asked, 'What else are we expecting today?'

'There's an emergency cesarean section going on right now on a twenty-eight-year-old female with pregnancy-induced hypertension—her blood pressure is unbelievably high. We also have a hysterectomy scheduled on a forty-seven-year-old woman with chronic pelvic inflammation and our orthopedic man is pinning an eighty-year-old man's hip—the old guy apparently fell out of his wheelchair at the nursing home.'

'Anything else?'

'There are a number of consultations and Kim has several abnormal pap smears to review.'

'Fine. I want you to schedule a meeting with all the pathology and clinical lab staff this afternoon at fourteen hundred hours.'

'I'll have *Emily* spread the word,' she replied, trying hard not to take offense at his order or his crisp manner. If he thought she would serve as his personal assistant, he could think again.

'Of course. I should have realized that.'

'We also have a policy that meetings must be posted at least two days in advance so that everyone has the opportunity to see the announcement and make arrangements to attend.'

'I don't think anyone will mind the short notice this

time, do you, Doctor?' Although he appeared congenial, he quirked one eyebrow as if daring her to challenge his decision.

Heather gritted her teeth. He obviously didn't care how they'd done things in the past. 'Probably not. If you'll excuse me, I'll see to it,' she said before leaving the room at a fast clip.

Aaron wondered if she knew how much more attractive she became when her eyes were flashing. He knew she didn't appreciate the deviation from standard protocol, but he had to establish his authority early on, regardless of how unpopular that might make him. The procedures and work he'd seen this morning seemed in line with standard pathology practices, but it was too soon to dismiss Paul Carter's dire warnings. It might take several weeks for the staff to slip back into sloppy habits if they were so inclined.

Somehow he wasn't surprised that Heather had enthusiastically embraced meeting the patients whose lives depended on her diagnosis. Isolated in laboratories, pathologists passed judgment on healthy or diseased lumps of tissue, easily forgetting the people whom those specimens represented. She had obviously chosen a path ensuring that she didn't fall into the inherent trap of her occupation.

Perhaps Paul Carter's hints of the department needing guidance and direction stemmed from disapproval of her nonconformity rather than concern over her expertise. If so, Carter's warnings meant that she'd probably had other innovative ideas—ideas that he opposed. Appreciating originality, Aaron couldn't wait to dig deeper into the situation. He loved to champion the underdog—and the dazzling smile that she'd bestowed on him after he'd agreed that she could continue her biopsy patient visits would serve as his incentive.

Drumming the fingers of his left hand on the counter, he flipped through manuals with his right. He judged the paperwork to be in order, although something he couldn't quite pinpoint bothered him. As he continued with his offhanded perusal, his thoughts turned to his new office.

Although it was smaller than what he was used to, he still found places for most of his personal touches: his medical-school diplomas, two family pictures, a desk set from his wife on the Christmas before they were married. Limited wall space kept him from hanging the New England covered bridge painting that Josh had selected at a flea market, but the plants compensated for the loss. He wondered who'd had the idea to suspend the glass hummingbird suncatcher among the greenery. It added a nice touch.

Idly, he turned another page—and froze. An intriguing detail popped out at him.

Laboratory standards were explicit—directors conducted annual policy and procedure reviews—and inspectors were notoriously obsessive about checking for compliance. So why would Dr Manning's signature—not Dr Walker's—appear on every document for the past three years?

'Dr Manning?' Melody inquired, peering into Heather's office. 'Dr Wheeler's sent Caitlin Burns over with more orders. You had mentioned you'd like to see her the next time she came in. Are you free now?'

'Of course.' Heather marked her place in the reference book and followed the young woman to the outpatient laboratory. There she saw a brown-eyed, pigtailed child wearing a pink flowered T-shirt and matching shorts.

'Hello, Caitlin. I'm Dr Manning. How are you today?'

'Fine,' the little girl replied, her smile showing off white baby teeth.

'Has Melody taken a blood sample from you yet?'

Caitlin nodded as her mother answered. 'Yes, and she didn't even cry—did you, sweetheart?'

She shook her head.

'Can I look at your arms, Caitlin?' Heather knelt down to be at the girl's level. The child thrust out both arms and Heather studied the tiny red spots dotting the skin. 'Can you tell if she's developing any more?'

'I don't think so,' Mrs Burns replied. 'Some are fading, though.'

'Thank you, Caitlin,' Heather addressed the tot before she rose.

'Dr Wheeler wants her to have a weekly blood test from now on,' Mrs Burns announced.

Heather nodded. 'We'll keep in close contact with him until we pinpoint the cause.'

'Do you think it could be——?'

The mother's anxious tone made her interrupt. 'It may not be anything serious, Mrs Burns, but it's better to check every possibility. Wouldn't you agree?'

'Yes.'

'I'll see you both next week.' Heather patted the child's shoulder, wishing she could offer the mother a more definite diagnosis. She knew, with a wordless glance at Melody, that the technologist would bring Caitlin's results to her as soon as they were available.

She returned to the histology lab, hoping Aaron had decided to spend some time in his office. Her hopes withered at the sight of the dark head studying the bound copies of past pathology reports.

'All done?' he asked, slamming the book closed and replacing it on a shelf.

'Yes. I got sidetracked with a patient.' She briefly explained Caitlin Burns' case.

'Sounds interesting. I'd like to be kept posted on anything unusual or interesting you find. Perhaps we could set aside a few minutes every day for that purpose?'

She bristled. Was this his way of checking her work? Darn it, she'd proven herself capable a long time ago. She didn't appreciate having to do it again. The idea of discussing her cases with him reminded her of her internship and residency.

'If you're not sure I'm capable——'

'I don't question your abilities, Doctor,' he interrupted calmly. 'I simply want to be aware of what's going on here. You aren't a one-man—or I should say one-woman?—operation anymore and it's a reasonable assumption that I may have to answer questions about one of your cases if you're unavailable.'

Duly chastised, she had to admit that his argument held a great deal of logic. 'I'm sorry for overreacting. You're right.'

'Now that wasn't so hard, was it?'

If he only knew, she thought.

'Breakfast was a long time ago. Shall we adjourn for lunch or do you skip that too?'

Heather's mouth turned up slightly. 'I didn't mean to make you miss your morning break. I have a tendency to bypass those.'

'Perhaps you won't need to any longer,' he replied, as if he'd understood that she used that time to keep from falling too far behind in her work.

After changing into fresh clothing, she guided him to the hospital cafeteria and then to the medical staff's dining room. There she pointedly introduced him as the new chief pathologist. When several physicians looked startled by her announcement, she smiled and pretended to be happy with the situation.

'You'll meet the majority of the doctors on Wednesday morning at our weekly staff meeting,' she said as they sat at a table with their dinner trays.

'Good.'

'You mentioned you accomplished a lot this weekend. Did you get everything unpacked?'

He shrugged his broad shoulders. 'Most of it. What's left can stay in boxes for a while.'

'Are you buying a house, or renting?'

'I bought it.'

So much for the idea that he'd go back to the East Coast. Her hopes nose-dived.

'I'm curious. What brings you to the central United States?' Heather cut her steak into tiny pieces, but left the meat on her plate.

'My son needed a different environment. Two boys had brought guns to school. Joshua happened to get caught in the middle and was shot——'

'Oh, my God,' she gasped.

'But luckily he only received a flesh wound. I considered another school in the area, but Josh was scared to leave the house. I thought I'd send him to a private boarding school, but when it came down to it I couldn't. My job at Bethesda Naval Hospital wasn't worth the guilt I felt. Luckily I ran across Plainview's advertisement before the application deadline passed.'

Lucky indeed, thought Heather.

'To make a long story short, the situation here seemed perfect for us, and here I am.'

To her, it seemed inconceivable that a man on the cutting edge of medicine in a well-known medical center would accept a position in quiet little Plainview. She wondered if he realized the culture shock both he and his son would experience.

'If you're thinking our educational facilities don't have problems, you're wrong,' she mentioned.

'I know. Drugs, alcohol and crime are everywhere. But Plainview's a small community and I'd like to think the odds of something terrible happening to Josh are small in comparison with those of a larger city.'

By the end of their meal break, Heather had decided to actively begin her job hunt since the Spences were in Plainview to stay.

In addition, she'd formed a completely different picture of her boss. As much as she wanted to, how could she dislike a man who cared for his son so much that he'd given up a prestigious career at one of the top medical centers in the country for his child's welfare?

'Since I've given you such short notice, I'll keep my remarks brief,' Aaron told the small crowd assembled in the laboratory's meeting room. 'I must admit, I've never addressed a standing-room-only group before.'

His remark brought chuckles and smiles to the thirty-odd individuals gathering in a room with accommodation for half that number. Heather, being one of those without a chair, leaned against the wall with her hands tucked behind her and smiled too.

'Since the hospital's rumor mill hasn't had much time to spread any information, I'd like to tell you a few things about myself,' Aaron began.

Her gaze flitted around the room. Everyone's eyes were trained on the new physician, each face etched with curiosity. Thankful that none of their expressions reflected boredom or even animosity, she let out a breath she didn't realize she'd been holding. She tuned into his conversation to catch the tail end of his sentence.

'. . .son, Joshua. We'd originally planned to arrive right before school started, but our house sold sooner than I'd anticipated. Luckily, your administration was amenable to my early arrival, so here I am.'

That explained why he'd appeared out of the blue, she thought.

He continued. 'I've been at a number of facilities, although most have been larger than Plainview. I spent the last seven years at Bethesda Naval Hospital in Maryland. In addition to my regular pathology duties, I headed a forensic pathology team to investigate air crashes. Even though I've moved here, I'm still a part of that group.'

Immediately Heather knew that Aaron would be summoned in the event of an air disaster. Once again she'd be left to shoulder the department's responsibilities—to assume command at a moment's notice and relinquish it just as quickly.

She pursed her lips, painfully aware that she'd have

to endure this experience over and over again if she remained at Plainview.

'Before I take any questions, I'd like to mention one thing. I dearly love homemade cinnamon rolls with my morning coffee.'

Everyone broke into laughter and she couldn't help but join in. It appeared that a fondness for food was a common trait among lab staff everywhere. Even if he hadn't mentioned his preference, he would have soon learned that rarely did a day pass without someone bringing goodies to share. It was a sure bet that cinnamon rolls would appear with much more frequency now.

'Dr Manning likes them too,' someone called out.

Aaron turned toward her for confirmation and she couldn't hold back a grin. He seemed almost pleased to hear that tidbit of trivia. Facing the group, he said, 'Then I'd have to say she has good taste.'

'What changes are you planning?' one of the supervisors asked.

'At the moment, none. But that's not to say there won't be some in the future. Needs change, and I think we should be flexible to meet those needs. But I'm also a firm believer in the adage if it ain't broke, don't fix it.'

Before the meeting disbanded, Heather noticed that the staff had acceptance written across their features. Aaron had done an excellent job of convincing them that they wouldn't experience any major upheavals for the time being.

Unfortunately, she didn't fall into the same category. His mere presence had shaken her world in earthquake proportions.

CHAPTER THREE

'MARTIN JENNER is a fifty-five-year-old Caucasian who called his doctor after running a fever for three days,' Heather reported to Aaron as they strode down the hall Tuesday morning. 'He doesn't complain of any specific symptoms, just a general tiredness. In every one of his cultures, our microbiology people have isolated only the normally occurring bacteria.'

'Anemia?' he asked, holding a door open and waiting for her to precede him into another long hallway.

'Yes, but it isn't severe enough to warrant a blood transfusion. His white blood cell counts are within our reference ranges, but they're at the low end of the scale. We've also seen a few immature cells that usually don't appear.'

'Preliminary diagnosis?' he asked.

'Something is definitely interfering with the normal function of his bone marrow since the three cell lines it produces are affected,' she replied promptly. 'But I'll defer my diagnosis until I have more data. I don't want to overlook anything because of a preconceived opinion.'

The pair approached the doorway labelled 'EMERGENCY' and she pushed on the swinging door marked 'IN'.

The registered nurse handed the pathologist a clipboard containing the man's records as she said, 'Good morning, Dr Manning. Mr Jenner is in room five.'

Heather headed in that direction and Aaron followed. 'If ER is too busy,' she told him in an aside, 'the nursing supervisor sends my bone-marrow patients to the one-day surgery floor.'

'What do you mean by *your* patients? Don't the physicians do this procedure?'

'Only a few. Our two internal medicine specialists usually take care of their own cases unless they're swamped. The rest of the doctors prefer to let me handle them. Everyone's happy with our arrangement and I can control the kind of specimens I receive.'

She knocked on the examination-room door, waited a few seconds, then walked inside. 'Mr Jenner? I'm Dr Manning, and this is Dr Spence. We'll be taking a sample of bone marrow from your hip, but first I'd like to examine you.'

Jenner's skin pallor came as no surprise—the man was anemic, with only ten grams of hemoglobin instead of the expected fourteen to sixteen grams found in males. While she palpated his abdomen, she quizzed him about medication and his occupation since certain drugs and workplace chemicals could induce the condition the man presented.

When she finished, she adjusted the top sheet. 'OK, Martin. We'll start in a few minutes.'

While the RN generously washed, shaved, then draped sterile towels over their patient's hipbone, Heather and Aaron followed their own sterilization procedures before donning gowns and surgical gloves.

A few minutes later, Heather swabbed the site with iodine and alcohol. 'I'm giving you a local anesthetic to take away most of the discomfort, but unfortunately you won't be totally pain-free. I know it won't be pleasant, but I'll do my best to finish as quickly as I can.'

Jenner nodded.

'Lidocaine,' she requested in a murmur and the nurse handed her a filled syringe.

After injecting the entire contents into the man's skin and muscle tissue, she made a small incision and wiped away the blood that appeared. She held out her hand and the nurse slapped the necessary instrument into her palm. 'You'll feel some pressure now.'

Using both hands and standing up for more leverage, she pushed the large marrow aspiration needle into the bone. Withdrawing the thin inner wire, she attached a syringe, then withdrew a few milliliters of precious marrow.

Aaron accepted the sample and skillfully prepared the necessary blood films, tissue imprints and culture specimens while she removed the stainless-steel apparatus and applied a pressure dressing over the wound.

'You'll need to rest here for at least an hour. If there isn't any bleeding, you can go home,' she advised.

'Thanks, Doc. I'm glad that's over.' Jenner wiped away the sweat on his upper lip with a shaky hand. 'How soon until you know something?'

'Your doctor will have our report no later than Thursday,' Heather promised before leaving.

'What's your opinion now?' Aaron asked as they left the emergency room.

'He denies taking any medication or dealing with hazardous chemicals, but he does have an enlarged spleen. I guess I'd lean more toward a leukemic condition.'

'From the look on your face during the exam, I

thought you'd found something. I'd have to agree with your diagnosis,' he said with a smile.

'We'll soon see if we're right or wrong.' She motioned to the tray of samples, feeling extraordinarily happy that they'd thought alike. Suddenly she wondered if they had other things in common. . . 'Do you like spicy food?' she blurted. 'There's a very good Mexican café on Third Street if you enjoy that type of cooking.'

'Do I ever,' he said fervently. 'And the hotter the better.'

She grinned. 'Some friends and I plan to go there tomorrow night. You and Josh are welcome to join us, if you'd like.'

Aaron accepted with enthusiasm. 'I never turn down an invitation for a meal I don't have to prepare. Our housekeeper in Maryland spoiled me, so my culinary skills are extremely basic.'

Encouraged by his positive response, she continued. 'In case you're interested, some of our local artists have an exhibit at the public library this month. The artworks they've donated for the hospital's annual benefit auction are on display, too.'

'I take it this is an event we're expected to attend?'

'Let's just say if you're not present Paul Carter expects an extremely good excuse. Something along the lines of coma or death. Your own, of course.'

'Of course,' he said, his mouth quirked into a half-grin. 'We must impress our benefactors. A dress-up affair, too, if I'm not mistaken?'

'You've been through this routine before,' she said knowingly. In the past, she'd attended the annual charity function under duress, leaving as soon as she could slip away. But now, enticed by an image of Aaron in black formal wear, she knew she wouldn't dread the evening or leave this year's gala before it ended.

'So when is this auspicious occasion?'

She thought a moment. 'In about six weeks. September fourteenth. So mark your calendar.'

'I will,' he promised. But before he could say anything else several people intercepted them.

'Dr Manning,' Kim said, 'I have several pap smears that need your review, and Larry called to say that he has Microbiology's monthly report for the pharmacy committee ready for your review.'

A blood-bank technologist voiced another message. 'A nurse in ICU wants to know if she can add saline to a unit of red cells so she can infuse it faster. I didn't know what to tell her.'

Heather started to answer, but before she uttered one word she saw Aaron's mouth straighten and his eyes turn cool and questioning.

'You aren't a one-man—or should I say one-woman?—operation anymore. . .'

With painful insight she realized she had to defer to his leadership. To do otherwise would be to pit herself and the staff in the middle of a power struggle she hadn't the slightest chance of winning. Emotionally, she felt bare, stripped of the authority she'd once enjoyed.

'Dr Spence?' She fastened her gaze on his, waiting for his decision.

Without breaking eye contact, he spoke. 'Why don't you deal with Intensive Care while I help Kim? The one who finishes first can handle Microbiology.'

She acknowledged his directive with a brisk nod before escaping into her office to call the intensive-care unit. After explaining that additional saline was unnecessary unless the patient was dehydrated, she headed for the microbiology section, still in a subdued frame of mind.

Luckily, Larry's report was only a few pages long and she quickly read through his findings and initialed the document. From there, she searched out Martin Jenner's stained-bone-marrow films in the cytology lab.

Aaron's now familiar baritone drifted toward her from the adjoining room. She chided herself for her poor attitude. It was past time to accept the unpleasant circumstances that fate had thrust upon her and get on with her life. Nothing would be gained by concentrating on what she'd lost. She must forge ahead. With strengthened resolve, she answered the ringing telephone.

'Dr Manning? Judith Dalton's secretary called and wanted to know our plans for the county health fair since they're printing the publicity brochures next week.'

'You'd better talk to Dr Spence, Emily. He may have some ideas of his own.'

'OK.' Emily's drawn-out reply made it evident that she wasn't looking forward to the task.

'By the way, Doctor, your dad called. He'd like you to call him back ASAP. Oh, and don't forget Dr Franklin wants to see you upstairs.'

'Thanks for the messages, Em.' Knowing Richard Manning the Third as well as she did, Heather suspected that he'd demanded rather than requested a return phone call. At least with Janet's request for consultation she could keep the upcoming conversation to a minimum. She took a deep breath in the ensuing silence before punching out a long-distance number from memory.

Speaking of unpleasant circumstances. . .she thought, sighing.

'What's next?'

'That was the last slide, Dr Spence,' Kim announced, jotting their findings on a worksheet.

Aaron leaned back in his chair and crossed his arms. 'You have a good eye, Kim. You picked up a number of abnormalities that are easily missed.'

The redhead blushed. 'Thank you.'

'How's your workload? Too much to do in too little time?' He grinned as he repeated a familiar lament.

'Sometimes. Unfortunately we haven't reached the point where we can justify hiring another full-time cytotech. Dr Manning tried to persuade the budget committee to add a part-time position but they wouldn't approve it. They counterproposed a person on a stand-by basis, but we haven't found anyone willing to work under those conditions. Most people have bills to pay and they need a steady income.'

He nodded, understanding their dilemma. 'We'll have to keep our eyes and ears open. Maybe we'll hear of a housewife or a retiree who would like the extra money even if it comes sporadically.'

'Dr Spence?' A timid voice came from behind.

'Yes?' He swiveled his chair to greet the speaker and stifled the smile that threatened to spread across his face. Emily looked terrified.

'Dr Manning said I should ask you about the county health fair. It's coming up in three weeks and the administrator's office wants to know what we plan to do so they can prepare the announcements.'

'Oh. Well, what have you done in the past?' He steepled his fingers, not surprised that they'd consulted Heather first. After the episode in the hallway, it was obvious that it would take some time for everyone to become accustomed to his role in the department. At least Heather encouraged the staff to come to him. Her actions suggested that she was willing to turn the reins over to him without incident. Good thing, too. He'd rather do other things with his attractive colleague than squabble.

'We've had a booth in the city auditorium and distributed literature. We also offered cholesterol screening the last two years,' Emily reported.

'Sounds fine. Go ahead.' Thinking the matter settled, he clicked his pen and scribbled his signature on a report. Neither woman moved and he looked up, catching the distressed looks they exchanged. When Emily nibbled on her lower lip, he knew a problem lurked underneath the surface. 'Is anything wrong?'

'Not really, but. . .well. . .' Emily wrung her hands.

Aaron leaned back and stowed his pen in his shirt pocket. 'Yes?'

'I think Dr Manning wanted to do something different this year,' Kim blurted out.

'I see.' For some reason, the fact didn't surprise him. 'What did she have in mind?'

Emily spoke up, chatty now that Kim had opened the discussion. 'We'd talked about offering an anemia screen and that prostate antigen test. Of course, we'd still offer to check cholesterol levels for those who wanted it.'

He thought for a moment. The test menu sounded fine, especially the prostate specific antigen test. The PSA, as it was generally called, seemed to be gaining popularity because it often detected early stages of prostate cancer before symptoms even appeared.

'I don't have any particular objections, but I'll discuss the subject with Heather. How soon do you need to know?'

'In the next day or two,' Emily replied, her wrinkled forehead relaxing into a smooth line.

'Is she in her office? I'll talk to her right now.' He rose, ready to tackle the issue immediately.

'She was on her way to see Dr Franklin on Five South but stopped to return a phone call. Her father.'

Aaron heard the secretary whisper the last comment to Kim. Seeing their troubled faces once again, he drew his own conclusions. 'He's not a nice man, I take it?'

'The man wouldn't know "nice" if it bit him on the nose,' Emily declared. 'He visited here once and was just as cold and demanding as he is whenever he telephones. Dr Manning never says anything about him, but she gets real quiet after their conversations. How someone like him ended up with a sweet daughter like her I'll never know. He's probably chewing her out right now for——' Her palm flew to her mouth and her eyes widened with obvious distress.

'For what?' he prompted.

Both women fidgeted; Kim inspected her fingernails while Emily studied the floor.

'For what?' he repeated.

'For not getting Dr Walker's position,' Emily mumbled. 'That was her goal, you know.'

Silence reigned for several seconds. 'He surely realizes six months isn't very much experience,' he replied, sensing that he should tread lightly on the subject.

'Six months, my eye!' Kim scoffed. 'Heather's acted as the chief for longer than I care to remember. Why, she's so dedicated, she works ten-hour days nearly seven days a week.'

'What?' Although he'd seen evidence that she'd handled more responsibility than an assistant pathologist usually did, he was surprised to hear that she'd assumed those obligations so early in her career.

'Dr Walker had early stages of Alzheimer's,' Kim said flatly. 'A few months after Heather came, we noticed he'd do things like forget where he was going, or what he'd done. He started making mistakes—little ones at first, then. . .' She paused. 'It reached the point where Heather didn't trust anything he did. Some days he'd be fine and there wouldn't be any problems. Other days. . .' She shrugged.

'She convinced him to deal with administrative issues and leave the patient work for her to deal with,' Emily broke in. 'When he didn't come to work——'

'Which was fairly often,' Kim interjected.

'She covered for him,' Emily finished.

'Didn't Dr Carter or Ms Dalton know the situation?' He frowned, already guessing the answer.

'I don't think so,' Kim admitted.

'Why wouldn't she bring something that important to their attention?' he mused aloud.

'Dr Walker lost his wife a few years ago, and Heather originally thought his problems stemmed from grief. She did her best to help him, afraid that he'd lose his job before he could pull himself together.'

'He should have taken a leave of absence.'

Emily's curls bounced as she shook her head. 'I don't think he had the finances for an unpaid sabbatical. He had a lot of expenses associated with his wife's illness.'

'He functioned very well if someone asked a specific question, so Heather used him more as a consultant. She'd finally decided to talk with Dr Carter, but then Dr Walker had a heart attack. After that there didn't seem much point in bringing it up. . .' Kim's voice trailed away.

Aaron rubbed his chin. He wished Carter had mentioned that Heather had applied for the position. At least he understood now why everyone looked to her for guidance—they'd done so for such a long time that it was a deeply ingrained habit.

It also explained the bleak look on her face when she'd allowed him to decide how to handle the sudden influx of demands.

Suddenly, other things he'd heard took on new meaning: the surgeon offering congratulations, the looks of surprise on a few physicians' faces after his introduction, the harmless plots he'd overheard last Friday, Heather moving out of Walker's office.

'She doesn't want people to know, so you won't tell her we said anything, will you?' Emily asked, her eyes pleading.

'No,' he said slowly. 'But, between the three of us, I'm glad you did.'

Later, staring out of his office window, he knew what his own reaction would have been if the situation were reversed. He'd have been networking with friends and making contacts with other hospitals.

And if he accurately remembered the comment he'd overheard—'He'll be around for another ten or fifteen years—a lot longer than I will—Heather had already set her career wheels in motion.

'For coming back from a three-day weekend in the mountains, Janet, you don't look very rested,' Heather teased when she entered the glassed-in nurses' station to see her friend.

'Why is it that whenever I close my office for a few days I need three weeks to catch up again?' Janet Franklin grumbled goodnaturedly, looking up from the chart in front of her. 'Now I know why you chose pathology. No midnight calls about a kid's sore throat he's had for a week, no expectant mothers with babies anxious to appear at three a.m., no patients going into diabetic coma because they indulged their sweet tooth, no——'

Heather held up her hands and laughed. 'I get the picture. Bad couple of days, I take it?'

'That's an understatement. Anyway, thanks for coming.'

'No problem. What can I do for you?'

Janet passed her a record sheaf. 'I wanted to toss around some ideas about one of my patients with you since it's more in your area of expertise than mine, but I think I know what you'll tell me.'

'Let's hear it.' Heather leaned against the counter and crossed her arms over the chart pressed against her chest. She enjoyed working with Janet, not only because she was a sharp diagnostician, but because their personalities meshed so well. Janet's bubbly disposition offset Heather's more serious one, uplifting her spirits numerous times in the past. Their similar experiences in dealing with a height disadvantage cemented their friendship by giving them one more thing—besides medicine—in common.

'Mrs Reddig——' Janet motioned to the room directly in front of them '—is fifty-five and has a history of a cough that didn't respond to penicillin. She also has hypertension and underwent a coronary bypass three years ago. Her lung infection is improving, but she isn't responding as fast as I'd like. To compensate for the chronic anemia, we gave her two units of packed red cells.

'That was two weeks ago. Her hemoglobin has dropped down to seven grams and there aren't any indications that she's bleeding anywhere.'

Heather looked thoughtful and began flipping through the laboratory records. 'Her transfusion was uneventful?'

'No problems whatsoever.'

'She might be experiencing a delayed reaction. Since red cells survive for as long as three months, something is obviously destroying them before their time,' Heather remarked, perusing the latest report.

'That's what I thought, but I wanted your opinion.'

'Were you planning to order another crossmatch?'

'I have no choice.'

Heather jotted a few lines on her consultation form, snapped the folder closed and handed it back to Janet. 'I'd recommend you also order the tests I've listed. If your patient did have a reaction to the blood she received, the blood bank will find the cause with these procedures. If we don't have compatible blood in stock, we'll request what we need from the Red Cross. It may take an extra day or two, though.'

'No problem. Just let me know what you find.'

'Will do.'

'Would you like to see Mrs Reddig?'

Heather glanced in the room. The small figure under the sheet remained still. 'I don't want to wake her. I may stop in after we know more.'

'OK. Hey, are you still free for our dinner date tomorrow?' Janet asked.

'Naturally. You know I can't pass up Rosa's pork chili and guacamole dip.'

'Yeah, neither can Dave,' Janet said.

'Is it OK if Dr Spence and his son join us? Aaron said they both like Mexican-style cooking, and Josh is the same age as Kevin.'

'Oo, this sounds interesting,' Janet teased.

'Well, don't get excited,' Heather said drily. 'I simply invited them to join us since they don't know many people or their way around town.'

'Uh-huh.' Janet didn't sound convinced by her explanation, and Heather had to admit that it did seem lame. A town where a person could drive from the east end to the west in fifteen minutes—even if he hit every stoplight—hardly needed its residents giving guided tours to newcomers.

'So I had a weak moment,' she admitted, shrugging. 'Don't rub it in.'

Janet grinned. 'So how *is* this Aaron Spence?'

Heather tugged on her necklace. 'OK, I guess.'

'Is that good or bad?'

'I wish I knew.'

'What's he like?'

Heather blinked. 'He seems to be openminded about things. At least he hasn't made any drastic changes. Yet. The staff seem to like him, too. He came from

Maryland, you know. Joshua was shot while at school and Aaron wanted him in a different environment.'

'Oh, my. I would too.' Janet paused. 'But you're still sorry he came,' she stated softly.

'I know I shouldn't be but. . .' Heather twisted her pendant. 'I guess I'm worried he'll leave me holding the bag like Noah did.'

'What do you mean?' Janet lowered her voice.

Heather took a deep breath. 'He's part of a government pathology team that investigates air crashes. That isn't a job you fly into one day and go home the next. We're talking weeks on end. And while he's off identifying bodies and whatever else he has to do, who do you think will be here at home putting in the twenty-hour days and getting absolutely nothing for it?'

'I see your point. But maybe he won't be gone very often.'

'Maybe.' Heather was doubtful.

'I'm really sorry you didn't get Noah's job. You really deserved it, in more ways than one. How did your dad take the news?'

Heather felt Janet's gaze on her. 'He's not extremely happy with me,' she confessed. 'But he'll get over it sooner or later.' Just as I will, she added silently.

'What are you planning to do?'

'I've sent my curriculum vitae to a few places looking for a pathologist.'

'Dr Franklin, you're wanted in the labor room,' a nurse interrupted from the doorway.

'Thanks, Toni,' Janet answered, then turned back to her friend. 'Promise me one thing, Heather.'

Heather cocked her head and waited expectantly.

'Don't rush into another job just to please your dad. Take your time. Make certain it's really what you want.'

'I will.'

No, she wouldn't grab at just any position that came along—she could afford to be selective. But she wouldn't wait for a job that was too perfect to exist, either.

'You're back,' a masculine voice stated from the doorway.

'A few minutes ago. Come on in.' Heather leaned around the microscope standing on one corner of her desk to click off the radio. Knowing Aaron would find the Reddig case interesting, she commented without preamble, 'We may have a delayed TR upstairs.'

'Really?' He lounged in the small chair wedged between her desk and the filing cabinet.

She recited the details. 'I've alerted the blood bank and the tech will let me know what she finds.'

'Good. Incidentally, Emily mentioned that we need to present our health fair plan no later than tomorrow. PSAs and hemoglobin levels, to be exact.'

'Yes, but if you'd rather we offer the usual cholesterol checks——'

'I don't think so,' he cut in. 'PSAs are a hot news item right now since several celebrities have admitted the test saved their lives.'

'True.'

'Do we need to obtain approval to cover the cost?'

'Oh, no,' she assured him. 'Those individuals who participate in the screening pay the price of the tests they choose. Since the fair is a community service, the fee only covers our expenses.'

'What happens to the results?'

'We send copies to the patient and to his or her personal physician. For those with an abnormal report, we also include a letter encouraging them to see their family doctor. In the case of the PSAs, I thought it would be worth our time to give a verbal notification also.'

He looked thoughtful, then nodded. 'OK. It sounds like you've worked everything out, so let's go for it.'

'Wonderful.' Heather couldn't help the smile that spread from ear to ear. She'd mentioned her ideas to Dr Carter a few weeks ago to get his input, and he'd wanted the lab to stick to the more traditional cholesterol screening. It was so nice to work with someone willing to try new ideas.

'I appreciate Emily asking for my decision. I hope she learned that I don't bite.' He grinned.

'Except when your knee bothers you,' she reminded.

His deep, hearty laugh filled the room and she prayed she'd hear it often.

'Touché,' he answered. Looking over his surroundings, he grimaced. 'No offense, but this is a claustrophobic person's nightmare.

'I prefer to call it cozy.'

'Working alone, you probably didn't spend much time in here.'

'No, I didn't. I was either in the lab or in—er—Dr Walker's office.'

'Of course.'

'He had the better microscope,' she defended.

'I believe you. But tell me something. Were you expecting to advance into Dr Walker's position?'

Heather tugged on her necklace, focusing on his nose

rather than his blue eyes. She might have known he'd either hear rumors or draw his own conclusions. 'All the signs pointed in that direction.'

'I'm sorry you weren't chosen. I think you would have done very well,' he said softly.

She shrugged. His high opinion, though welcomed, changed absolutely nothing.

'I've spot-checked the lab's records covering the last few years. I *know* what you've accomplished, Heather. I'm just sorry no one else does.'

'It was my own fault. I should have reported him to the Medical Executive Committee, but I couldn't. Noah Walker needed us as much as we needed him.'

'I'll do whatever I can to help you get a chief's appointment at another hospital, even call in a few favors,' he promised.

Stunned by his offer, she froze.

Why was he being so helpful? Did he want her to leave?

CHAPTER FOUR

'WHY? You hardly know me.' Heather spoke bluntly.

'Not well, no. But your staff do and their loyalty speaks volumes. Coupled with the work I've seen, I don't have any qualms about putting in a good word for you.'

She fingered her necklace, startled as much by his praise as by his offer. Dropping the metal, she clasped her hands in her lap and looked directly at him.

'Thanks, but no, thanks. I prefer to be hired on my own efforts.'

'I understand. I felt the same way.'

Heather sensed he was pleased with her answer, although she didn't understand why. Aaron's casual acceptance of her decision contrasted with her father's aggressive reaction to the same news. The elder Manning's most recent conversation had centered on the leads he'd obtained from friends, and he'd vocalized at great length his opinions as to which one she should choose.

'But Dad,' she'd said, 'I don't want you to find a job for me. I want to get it myself. I want to be chosen because of my accomplishments, not because I'm your daughter.'

'I can't believe you'd be so ungrateful, Heather. There are physicians out there who would jump at the chance to have an edge.'

'That may be, but I'm not one of them,' she'd

insisted. 'I've already sent out several inquiries and I want to hear from them before I make any more.'

'Suit yourself. But if you're stuck in that hospital on the edge of nowhere for the rest of your life, don't come crawling to me.'

'I won't,' she'd promised, knowing his grudging surrender wouldn't last long. If her luck held, she might have an entire month's reprieve before he resumed his arguments.

Aaron's baritone pulled her attention into the present. 'Have you seen Jenner's bone-marrow slides yet?'

She grasped at the topic change with relief. 'I'm scanning them right now. From what I've seen so far, I'd say he's on the verge of developing leukemia. It's a textbook case of a pre-leukemic syndrome. I'm waiting for Kim's special stains before I confirm it.'

'Do we have an oncologist on staff?' he asked.

'In a manner of speaking. Dr Evans travels from sixty miles away several times a week. It saves the patients driving so far to receive their chemotherapy.' She sighed. 'It's a shame. Jenner seems like such a nice fellow.'

'Don't lose hope. The latest reports show that complete remission rates are rising.'

'I know.'

'Anything new on the Burns case?'

Heather shook her head. 'No change in her CBC. She'll be back again next week.'

'Maybe you should strongly consider a bone-marrow exam.'

'It's only been two weeks. I'd like to wait a little longer.'

'How much longer?'

His persistence suddenly made her aware that he had more than a casual interest in this particular case. Since she was the pathologist Dr Wheeler had consulted, Caitlin Burns was technically her patient. And since she hadn't asked for advice. . . She eyed her superior. 'I don't know. A week or two.'

'Hmm.'

'You'd recommend the exam *now*?'

'Probably.'

'Why?' She couldn't believe he'd opt for such an aggressive strategy.

Aaron shrugged. 'I prefer to take the offensive. If the patient is on the fringes of some deadly disease, I want to know about it. Early detection and treatment is the key, you know.'

'I'm aware of that fact,' Heather replied, her jaw clenched. 'I just don't want to put that child through a painful procedure unless it's absolutely necessary.'

'Neither do I, but you can't afford to be soft-hearted in this business. Your patients, especially Caitlin, can't afford it.'

'I think I'm being cautious, not soft-hearted,' she informed him, foreseeing problems arising over the differences in their philosophies.

'There's nothing wrong with caution,' he said. 'As long as you don't lose sight of the fact that not making a decision is making a decision of another sort.'

He rose to his feet, signifying that he considered the subject closed. 'I suppose it's time to call it a day. Is there anything I should be aware of before the staff meeting tomorrow?'

'No, but Dr Carter will probably ask you to say a few words.'

'I can handle that.'

After yesterday's lab meeting, I'm sure you can, she thought. Ill at ease with public speaking herself, she'd observed the smooth delivery of his informal address with respectful awe and a measure of jealousy. After all, the ability to capture an audience's attention— whether it consisted of one person or a roomful— played a significant role in most success stories.

If only she possessed half of his talent. . .

The following evening, Heather studied her reflection in her full-length bedroom mirror, wondering if she should change into dressier clothing. Dining out with her boss, even in the company of old and good friends at a casual restaurant, seemed to warrant something more classy than jeans.

A zipper-pull later, she stepped out of them. Tugging a straight denim skirt over her hips, she assured herself that comfort had dictated her choice—it was much cooler to have bare legs in ninety-degree summer heat—rather than a desire to impress Aaron. Smoothing the fabric, she scrutinized the reflected image. The below-the-knee hemline had added a stylish touch to the jade T-shirt with its handpainted Native American design. A satisfied smile appeared before she turned away to select coordinating jewelry.

It was ridiculous to be so nervous, she thought as she wandered into the living room to find her sandals. But she was, and had been all day. Especially since Aaron had caught her off guard with his invitation.

'I'll stop by your house at six-thirty,' he'd announced after their afternoon meeting.

'That isn't necessary,' she'd protested.

'No, but I'd like to.'

Heather frowned at the memory, unconsciously duplicating her expression during the hours-old conversation. 'I can meet you——'

'Nonsense. There's no need for you to drive when Josh and I come right past your house.'

'Well, if you're certain,' she'd acquiesced.

Recalling his satisfied smile, she scolded herself for giving in to his suggestion so easily. Admit it, a little voice taunted, this is the closest you've come to a date in a long time.

It was true. She hadn't been out with an eligible male for anything other than business since before her surgery. And that was more years ago than she cared to count.

The doorbell chimed and she opened the door.

'Hi,' Aaron said. A boy stood next to him, a gangly youth already taller than Heather. She knew she wouldn't have had any trouble identifying Aaron Spence's son in a room full of twelve-year-olds. He had his father's jawline and the same slate-blue eyes.

'Hi,' she greeted. 'Let me grab my purse, and then I'm ready.'

Slinging it over one shoulder, she stepped on to the porch and locked the door. Turning to Aaron's son, she stated with a smile, 'You must be Josh.'

The boy nodded, his face turning pink. 'I'm pleased to meet you, Dr Manning.'

'Please call me Heather.' Then, 'I don't know about you but I'm starved. Shall we go?'

Josh's face lit up. 'You bet,' he said, spinning round and heading for the car.

'I'm sorry we're late,' Aaron interjected, following

her down the sidewalk. 'We had a little trouble with the hot-water heater.'

'A leak?' she asked, conscious of his hand at the small of her back.

'A too small capacity,' he corrected her, looking at his son fondly. 'I either need to invest in a larger model or race Josh to the shower. How one boy can use that much water. . .' He shook his head and opened the car door.

Heather chuckled and slid inside as gracefully as one could with a tight skirt. Although the front slit only exposed her leg a few inches above the knee, she somehow felt as if a great deal more had been revealed. Perhaps she hadn't made such a wise choice after all.

A few minutes later and without asking for directions, Aaron approached the flashing sign proclaiming 'Rosa's'. As he turned into the parking lot, she joked, 'For being new in town, you know your way around very well.'

'I've been coached,' he admitted.

'Obviously,' she retorted.

While Josh hopped out of the car and she fumbled for the door handle, Aaron walked round to her side. Wordlessly he held out his hand. She laid her palm on his, accepting his help so that she could exit with dignity. Although he seemed to take the brief contact in his stride, she felt warm goose bumps even after the connection had been broken.

'Dad and I got a city map and we've been studying it,' Josh mentioned, hurrying ahead of them to the restaurant entrance. 'We drove around last night and found all the important stuff: the movie theater, the skating rink, and the miniature golf course.'

Heather chuckled. 'Ah. Plainview's cultural high points?'

'We also located the school and a church,' Aaron remarked drily, holding Rosa's door open. 'As you may have guessed, Josh doesn't include them on his list of significant places to visit.'

'Oh, Dad,' the youth moaned.

A hostess wearing a flowered skirt and peasant blouse appropriate for the atmosphere greeted them with a smile. 'Good evening, Dr Manning. Your party is waiting.'

'Thanks, Maria,' she acknowledged.

'I didn't realize you were so popular,' Aaron remarked, falling into step behind Heather.

'I'm not. The Franklins and I have a standing reservation for Wednesday night so the help knows us.'

'Let me guess. You don't need a menu.'

She laughed, feeling his hand resting on her back again and enjoying it. 'I don't even have to order.'

Maria led them to a table for six in a secluded corner. 'Hi, guys,' Heather said, seeing her friends already munching on a huge bowl of tortilla chips and salsa. 'Kevin, I'd like you to meet Joshua Spence. He'll be in your grade at school this fall.'

Amid a chorus of 'No kidding!' and 'Great!' Josh chose a seat close to his new acquaintance. She noticed the animated look on the boy's face, then glanced at Aaron. His eyes signaled his thanks and she congratulated herself for her foresight in requesting Kevin's presence.

As soon as the waitress had taken their orders, Josh turned to his father. 'Dad, can I borrow some money? Kevin and I want to play the video games.'

Aaron shifted his weight and leaned toward Heather in order to draw his billfold out of his hip pocket. The aromas of peppers and onions drifting out of the kitchen couldn't compete with his familiar spicy scent. Enjoying the contrast, she made no attempt to give him more maneuvering space. His shirt sleeve brushed against her bare arm and she felt a rush of awareness leap through her body faster than she'd ever imagined possible.

'How much do you boys need?' he asked, pulling out several small-denomination bills.

'I have my own money, Dr Spence,' Kevin replied.

Aaron handed the currency to Josh.

'Thanks, Dad.' Josh's eyes gleamed.

'Remember, this is only a loan,' he cautioned.

'I know. I'll pay you back when I get home,' Josh called over his shoulder, hurrying with his new friend to the bank of arcade machines.

Aaron returned the billfold to his pocket. Heather felt oddly bereft when she could only detect the typical Mexican restaurant odors.

'Thanks for bringing Kevin along,' he told the Franklins. 'I'm hoping Josh will find a few friends during what's left of the summer. I don't want him to feel so out of place when school starts in a few weeks.'

'No problem. I'm glad Heather suggested it,' Dave replied.

'The principal told me the classes aren't big,' Aaron commented.

'About twenty-five students per teacher, give or take a few,' Janet answered. 'Heather told me about his injury. You must have been devastated.'

'That's not an experience I'd wish on any parent. To be in the middle of what seems a perfectly normal day and be told your child has been shot, not knowing any details except he's on the way to the hospital. . . Was it minor, or was he dying. . .?' Aaron's voice sounded far-off, almost as if he was reliving the moment.

Heather covered his hand with hers and squeezed gently. He looked at her. His tentative smile, for some strange reason, made her glow inside.

After a few seconds of silence, he cleared his throat and turned his gaze on to his other dinner companions. 'Josh withdrew after it happened. Seemed afraid to be around large groups of kids. The school counselor said it was normal, and to give him time, but it didn't seem to help. I'm hoping the change of scenery will.'

'Does he participate in any sports?' Janet asked.

Suddenly aware that her hand still rested on Aaron's, and that Janet had seen her impulsive gesture, Heather quickly reached for a chip and dipped it into the salsa.

Aaron nodded. 'Track and field.'

'Really? Same as Kevin. He's a better long-jumper than runner, though. He placed second in the state's Hershey track meet a few weeks ago,' Dave announced proudly.

'Josh loves to run. After the accident he'd attend practices, but refused to compete.'

'If their friendship continues, his attitude may change,' Heather mentioned, nodding in the boys' direction. They were slapping their hands together high above their heads, obviously celebrating a victory.

'Broke already?' Aaron asked when the boys approached moments later.

'Naw, just hungry.' Kevin grabbed a handful of chips.

'Besides, some other kids wanted to play,' Josh answered. In spite of his seemingly magnanimous gesture and nonchalance, Heather noticed that he paid wary attention to the three boys who now hovered over the games machine. Aaron hadn't exaggerated Josh's phobia. He was clearly afraid.

At that moment their food appeared.

'Aaron, I can't tell you how glad I am that Heather isn't our only pathologist,' Janet said. 'Do you know she hasn't taken a real vacation for ages?'

'I have too,' Heather protested. 'I was gone for a week last March.'

Janet waved her hand, dismissing Heather's comment. 'I'm not talking about conferences. I'm talking about a real, genuine, bona fide vacation.'

Dave leaned toward Aaron and winked at Heather. 'You'll have to watch her; she has a habit of working above and beyond the call of duty. Last year she had bronchial pneumonia and refused to miss a day.'

'Hey, we've all been guilty of putting our patients ahead of ourselves,' Heather interjected, uncomfortable under Aaron's piercing scrutiny. Trying to minimize the impact of Dave's remarks, she added, 'Besides, I wasn't *that* sick.'

'Yeah, right,' Janet retorted.

'I'm sure we can rectify the situation,' Aaron said.

'Has she told you about Plainview's annual hospital benefit?' Janet asked.

Aaron nodded. 'An art auction, if memory serves.'

'Along with dinner and dancing. You do dance, don't you?' Janet's innocent-sounding question didn't fool Heather. Her friend's favorite hobby was matchmaking and unless Heather steered her in another direction Janet would plan their evening right down to the goodnight kiss. It was so typical of her to launch her campaign the same second that Heather took a huge bite of her taco salad. She chewed frantically but the meat and lettuce seemed to grow larger.

'I can hold my own,' Aaron replied.

'Wonderful,' Janet beamed. 'Heather always leaves early, but maybe this year you can convince her to at least stay until ten o'clock.'

'I'll see what I can do.' Aaron's amusement rang out and Heather finally swallowed the lump in her mouth.

'I don't think——' she began.

Janet's pager beeped. With a wink, and looking extremely satisfied, she excused herself and went to the nearby telephone.

Heather took another bite, vowing to have a few words with her friend at the earliest private opportunity. So she was attracted to Aaron. There was no need to coerce him into acting as her escort just because she'd grasped his hand in a weak moment. If—and she meant *if*—he agreed to accompany her, she wanted him to do so because he wanted to, not out of some sense of obligation.

'No problems,' Janet announced when she returned a minute later, answering everyone's silent query.

To Heather's relief, conversation during the rest of their meal dealt with the more mundane aspects of Plainview living.

'Mom, Dad, since it's still early, can Josh come to our house for a while? He'd like to see my bug collection,' Kevin wheedled, hope written across his face as the group rose to leave.

'No problem, as long as his dad doesn't mind,' Dave answered.

'Can I, Dad? Can I?' Josh pleaded.

'Only for about an hour,' Aaron conceded.

'Don't worry about Josh. We'll bring him home. Feel free to do something special,' Janet offered, winking at Heather.

Heather desperately wanted to pinch her friend. One would have to be deaf, dumb and blind not to see through her ploy, and Aaron was anything but.

'Thanks, I appreciate it.'

After settling their bills and a chorus of goodbyes, Heather and Aaron walked the length of the parking lot to his Audi. 'I can understand why you have a standing reservation here,' he remarked, unlocking the passenger door. 'The food was outstanding.'

'Better than you'd find in the city?' she teased.

'Much better.'

All too quickly, he parked in front of her house and stopped the engine.

Heather wondered if she should invite him in. It might appear as if she considered the evening a date, rather than a friendly get-together. Handsome fellow and great dinner companion that he was, Aaron was also her boss. Too bad, too. Although the idea of a romantic interlude with him sent her heart pounding, it was best that she get her imagination—and hormones—under control.

With that admonition, she couldn't believe she heard herself say, 'Would you like to come inside for coffee?'

'I'd love to.'

They strode up the curved cement pathway to the front entrance and a few moments later crossed the threshold. 'Make yourself at home,' she suggested before disappearing into the kitchen. Almost immediately she stuck her head around the corner. 'Is decaff OK?'

'At this time of day, it's perfect.'

She measured out the coffee grounds and filled the automatic drip reservoir with water, wondering the entire time what he thought of her home—her proverbial pride and joy.

Aaron was envious. An assortment of green foliage populated the area in front of a huge bay window, strategically placed to capture the morning sun. The lush growth made him miss the conservatory he'd added on to his home in Maryland where he'd indulged his green thumb. Now he knew where the plants gracing his office had originated.

He rarely entered a house and instantly felt comfortable, but he did with Heather's. He first attributed it to the light streaming through the airy curtains, making the room seem warm and personable while giving the occupants a sense of privacy at the same time.

Then again, perhaps he felt at home because she obviously loved books as much as he did. 'I see you like to read,' he called out.

Her words floated toward him. 'You bet. I can't pass a bookstore without buying something.'

Crossing the room to reach the north wall, he recognized extensive collections of mystery and adventure novels by his own favorite authors of Tom Clancy, Robert Ludlum and Robin Cook. He crouched down to scan the three lower shelves of the tall, tightly packed bookcase. Unfamiliar with the works by a variety of writers such as Amanda Quick, Scotney St James and Diana Palmer, he pulled out a thin volume by Renee Roszel. He smiled when he realized they were all samples of romantic fiction. Replacing the book, he rose and continued to study the room.

The different-textured furnishings seemed to beg for his touch, from the smooth Lladro figurine to the nubby weave of the sofa and needlepointed footstool. He liked that, deciding that Heather was a tactile sort of person.

The only oddity, if it could be called that, was the lack of personal memorabilia. Unlike his own living room where several photos of Josh and himself were prominently displayed, Heather's single photograph of a distinguished-looking older man stood half hidden behind a cactus.

But what kept his feet planted and his attention riveted were the three west windows he considered a masterpiece in stained glass.

He stood in front of them, studying the trio's detail. Sunbeams made a gorgeous array of rainbow-colored flowers in various shapes and sizes on the floor. He reached out, unable to stop himself from feeling the various textures of the leaded glass. If he hadn't guessed that she loved sunshine from the way she avoided her dark little office, he certainly knew it now.

She walked forward. 'What do you think?' she asked, thrusting her hands into her pockets and balling them into fists. His opinion suddenly seemed important.

Without tearing his gaze away from the glass picture, he gestured, 'This is absolutely beautiful.'

She relaxed her hands. 'Thank you. My artist friend helped me.'

'*You* did this?'

She grinned. 'Why does everyone sound surprised when I mention it? Can't doctors be artistic?'

'Oh, it isn't that.' He shook his head. 'It just seems like such a massive undertaking for a hobby project.'

'It was, although I have to admit if I hadn't had expert help and advice I wouldn't have attempted it at all. Even so, it took a lot longer than I'd anticipated. But it was worth it.'

'This is really impressive.' He cocked his head to study it from another angle.

'I'm glad you like it.' She heard the coffee maker sputter a last gasp of water and steam. 'The coffee's ready. Cream or sugar?'

'Sugar, please. One teaspoon.'

He followed her into the kitchen. His fingers brushed against hers as she passed the steaming drink prepared to his taste. Heat totally unrelated to the brew's warmth skittered up her arm and made her feel as if her internal temperature had risen well above 98.6.

'What a view,' Aaron declared, staring through the patio door into her backyard.

'Thanks.' Feeling like a proud parent, Heather knew that her yard, landscaped with evergreen shrubs, oak, maple and a few fruit trees, provided a restful haven after long, busy days. At one end, a small bridge arched over a pool. 'Would you like to sit outside or do you prefer air-conditioned comfort?'

'After you,' he quipped, gesturing toward the doorway with his mug. Descending the three steps on to the bricked patio, he went on, 'I see you have a herb garden.'

'The previous owners started it. I only recognize a few plants—the mint and the dill. The rest are a complete mystery.'

'I had a conservatory added to my house and I dabbled with herbs, among other things.'

'Really?' That explained his calluses and why he knew so much about plants.

'You have a nice variety—tarragon, sweet basil, thyme, anise, and parsley.' He touched each plant with gentle fingers as he identified it.

When he found the mint, he broke off a few leaves and handed one to her before chewing on his own.

Although she'd plucked mint leaves and brought them inside to sweeten the air, she'd never *eaten* them. But since he *did* seem to know what he was doing. . . Heather imitated him.

'Oh, my,' she said, surprised at the cool, fresh taste bursting across her mouth. She looked at his lips, suddenly overcome with a desire to learn how the smell of mint mingled with his masculine scent.

'Your plants are very healthy-looking.' Aaron's casual statement brought her back to reality and she focused her eyes on the foliage instead of the man.

'Do you think so? Emily has a book on herbs she said she'd loan to me.' She hurried on, hoping he wouldn't recall Emily's herbal reference from their first meeting. 'They haven't been getting much care. I hate to do anything until I know what I'm doing. Any suggestions?'

Aaron crouched down and dug in the topsoil with his free hand. 'Thin them out and cut down on the water. If you like, Josh and I can come over sometime and help.'

'Oh, would you?'

He rose and brushed his fingers against his trouser leg. 'No problem. Just say when.' Moving along the boundaries of her property, he asked, 'How do you find time to take care of all this?'

Heather walked beside him. 'I don't. A mom and pop lawn service do the dirty work. I kick up my feet and enjoy the scenery.'

They stopped at the pond. 'Goldfish?'

She chuckled at his surprise. 'I understand they do quite well outdoors, although this is my first try. I'll probably move them into an aquarium or give them away when winter comes.'

He scanned the yard again. 'Hmm. This is perfect for entertaining and family get-togethers.'

She ignored the latter half of his comment. 'The parties I host are on a very small scale.'

'What about your family?'

She sipped her now lukewarm drink. 'There's only my father and he doesn't visit very often.'

'Is that his photograph in your living room?'

'Yes. It was taken shortly after I graduated from medical school, a few years before I came to Plainview.'

'Our house is full of pictures. Although we haven't done it yet, Josh and I usually pick one wall and literally cover it with framed photos and snapshots.'

'Really?'

He nodded. 'The Spence family history, complete with grandparents and great-grandparents, is chronicled in that space. Josh is in the majority of them, although there are a few from my grade-school days. We have a lot of happy memories hanging there—a few sad ones, too.'

He became quiet and Heather suspected that he was thinking of those years immediately following his wife's death. She knew exactly how the pain of loss marked those supposedly happy occasions for a long time. Her own photos—few in number after her mother's death—were arranged in an album that was stuffed in a drawer and rarely opened.

'Your father must be very proud of you,' Aaron commented. 'You're a physician, plus you have a remarkable artistic talent.'

She swallowed hard, tugging on her necklace. How could she explain that nothing she did ever seemed to satisfy him? That deep down she understood why Richard Manning the Third wanted his daughter to fulfill the career dreams he'd lost through no fault of his own?

'He's never seen my stained glass. He wouldn't understand my need to express myself in that manner.'

Aaron shook his head. 'If Josh created something like you have, I'd drag people in off the street to look at it.'

Sensing rather than seeing his curiosity, she explained. 'My dad is very goal-oriented. If he knew what I did in my spare time, infrequent though it is, he'd croak.' She could hear his harsh voice now. 'Dabbling in art isn't the way to achieve your objective, Heather. Becoming chief pathologist requires hard work and discipline.'

A familiar ache grew in her stomach. Did she really want to pay the price? Did she want to go through the rest of her life like her father, never seeing the beauty around him in his haste to make an indelible mark on the world?

'What does he do?'

'He was a pathologist in Boston. A year after I graduated we were going home after the hospital

Christmas party—I was driving—when someone ran a red light and broadsided us. The accident left him a paraplegic, and injured his hands. He worked for a while, until arthritis made it impossible.' She ran her finger round the bottom edge of her mug.

'I'm sorry. And you?'

'A few scratches.'

'Your mother?'

'She died when I was seven; she had breast cancer. After that it was my father, me and whoever happened to be the current housekeeper.' A wan smile flitted across her face. 'We went through a lot of them.'

Wanting to turn the conversation away from herself, Heather asked, 'What about *your* housekeepers? Didn't you mention that one spoiled you?'

Aaron chuckled. 'Hattie Brewster. She hated the name Hattie and since Mr Brewster left her during what she called his male mid-life crisis she hated that name too. So we called her Mrs B.'

'How long did she work for you?'

'She was part of our family,' he corrected her. 'She joined us during Barbara's pregnancy and never left. Since Josh had no grandparents, she stepped into that role nicely, too.'

'Didn't she want to move here with you?'

'Yes, but she has two children and three grand-children she hated to leave behind. But I know she'd be here on the next plane if I asked her.'

They fell into an easy silence. Heather contemplated the contrast between Aaron's life and hers. Her father would never have treated the hired help as anything but servants, and none of them would have resumed their employment once they'd resigned. She couldn't help an age-old question surfacing. What made one man turn into a cold, heartless creature after the death of a spouse, while another seemed to accept his lot, pick up the pieces and continue?

Aaron drained the last drop of his coffee and pulled himself upright. 'I suppose I'd better find my way home before Josh does.'

'Of course.' She jumped to her feet, ready to escort him to the front door.

As they retraced their steps through her house, she realized how nice it felt to have a male medical professional—other than Dave—consider her hobbies and interests worthy of merit. A bittersweet pang shot through her at the thought of the evening ending.

His warm body, only a few inches away, generated a heat inside her that the cool room air couldn't dispel. The same worries that had struck her when he'd driven her home struck again. Should she shake his hand or avoid the brief contact altogether? Remembering his touch—and craving a repeat—sent pleasant shivers dancing down her spine.

He paused at the doorway. 'I had a nice time tonight, Heather. Thanks for inviting us.' Looking down at her, he took a half-step closer.

Instinctively, she sensed what was coming, and it wasn't a platonic handshake. She knew a kiss would be foolhardy, but didn't care. Not moving either forward or backward, she waited. Her skin tingled in anticipation, and her nostrils breathed in his familiar and pleasant odor. Eager, she tipped her head back to stare into his face. His slate-blue eyes flashed like sparkling waves of deep blue ocean. She licked her lips, savoring the mint. His would taste the same, she knew, yet somehow different.

He growled. A split second later his mouth brushed against hers, his arms enfolding her in a loose embrace.

She melted. The feel of his hard body against hers, his broad back underneath her hands, made her glad she hadn't settled for a casual goodbye gesture. His unique male scent, his minty breath, the play of his firm muscles were everything she expected and more.

Her knees wobbled. As if sensing her weakness, he tightened his hold.

She heard a moan, and wondered if it had come from deep in his throat or from hers. But it didn't matter. Nothing mattered except the fire blazing a trail through her body.

All too soon, he pulled back, leaving her shaky and breathless and barely able to stand.

'Goodnight, Heather.' He caressed her cheek.

'Goodnight, Aaron,' she murmured when she found her voice a minute later. But he didn't hear her. He was gone.

Aaron drove home thinking he shouldn't have kissed Heather, but he couldn't help it. He'd wanted to indulge himself ever since he'd met her. Had it really been less than a week ago?

The evening had been an eye-opener and well worth sharing the first two hours with the Franklins. Lucky for him, Heather had invited him into her house after dinner. He'd learned a lot about his beautiful colleague.

One: she didn't like to talk about herself.

Two: she toyed with her necklace when she was nervous.

Three: to say she'd had a rotten childhood was being kind. She'd lost her mother at a young age and had had housekeepers come into her life as often as she'd changed her socks. No, life in the Manning household couldn't have been easy.

Four: she felt guilty over her father's accident. He suspected that the unfortunate incident provided Dr Manning with the means to bend Heather to his will. Was Heather's goal of obtaining a chief's position her own, or her father's?

Five: her father was a first-class bastard.

He parked the Audi in the garage moments before the Franklins pulled alongside the curb. Thank heavens Josh had found a friend; he needed one. He'd seen his son hightail it back to their table at Rosa's when those three boys had appeared, even though there'd been plenty of machines for all five of them to play at once.

God, he hoped moving to Plainview had been the right decision. Too late now for doubt to set in, he reminded himself. Everything would work out. It had to.

Aaron waved to the family, hearing the chorus of 'See you tomorrow' and 'I had a great time' from the two boys as Josh got out of the car.

'Making plans?' he asked, swinging his arm around to rest on Josh's shoulders.

'Yeah. We're going to ride our bikes in the morning and Kevin said he'd let me use his ticket to see the matinee. *Revenge of the Nerds* is playing and tomorrow's the last day. We can't miss it.'

'Heavens, no,' Aaron agreed, struggling to keep a straight face.

'I'm hitting the shower.'

'Again?' When had Josh willingly taken a shower—much less two in one day?

Joshua looked sheepish. 'We played football with Kevin's neighbors—they're twins—and I got a little dirty during some of the tackles.'

Aaron noticed the smudges on the boy's arms, and wiped away the one across Josh's right cheekbone. 'I'd say so,' he remarked. 'Try not to use all the hot water again.'

'OK.' Josh headed for the bathroom.

Aaron turned toward his study and smiled, considering Josh's participation in a four-man scrimmage a positive step. If his son needed the small town of Plainview to heal his emotional wounds, he wouldn't do anything to jeopardize their life here—namely, his job. And if that included keeping his relationship with Heather on a platonic basis, so be it. Even without the threat of a three-month probation—a mere formality—charges of sexual harassment would see his days numbered.

He turned his head and caught a lingering scent of Heather's perfume on his collar. 'On second thoughts, Josh, take your time,' he called out. An ice-cold shower suddenly seemed like a good prescription.

CHAPTER FIVE

'YOU'RE early today,' Heather remarked, meeting Janet in the physician's parking lot the next morning.

'Two of my mothers are in labor and I came by to check them before I open the office,' Janet replied. 'I can tell we're coming into a full moon. Babies are popping out all over the place.'

Heather smiled. 'And you're loving every busy minute.'

Janet grinned in wordless agreement. 'Anyway,' she continued, 'I'm glad I caught you. Have you found anything on Mrs Reddig?'

'Just as we'd suspected, the lady's having a delayed transfusion reaction,' Heather said, juggling her briefcase and a can of orange juice.

'No kidding?'

'No kidding,' Heather affirmed. 'The interesting thing is that her immune system is producing an autoantibody—a special protein—that is destroying her very own red cells. Hence the chronically low hemoglobin.'

'So what are my options?' Janet asked.

'We've requested three units of compatible packed red cells from the regional Red Cross facility. That should bring her hemoglobin to a more reasonable level.'

'Steroids?'

Heather shook her head. 'Not if she's still exhibiting signs of an infection. The best thing I can advise is to treat her with antibiotics—I know you are—and monitor her hemoglobin level.'

'Her case is unusual, isn't it?'

'Somewhat, but this condition isn't unheard of. I researched this problem last night and found a few articles linking her particular abnormality with a concurrent bacterial infection, just as you've reported. If you like, I can send you copies.'

'Thanks.' A lazy grin appeared on Janet's face and she winked. 'Now be honest. Did you by any chance have tall, dark and handsome help when you conducted your research?'

Heather rolled her eyes. 'Hardly. He left when Josh was due home.'

'Aha. So he *did* stay at your place for a while.'

'A very *short* while,' Heather corrected her. 'We sat outside, drank coffee and talked about my garden. So you can wipe that silly grin off your face. Everything was very innocent.' Except for the kiss.

Heather remembered that magical moment. It was too intense and much too special to share.

Janet nudged her friend. 'Something must have happened or you wouldn't look like you've just bitten into your favorite double chocolate fudge cheesecake. What was it?'

'Nothing. Nothing happened.'

Janet dismissed Heather's denial. 'Don't be ridiculous. You forget how well I know you.' Leaning closer, she whispered, 'He kissed you, didn't he?'

'Well. . .yeah.'

'Oh, I knew it,' Janet crowed.

Heather felt her face warm. The heat intensified when she saw Janet's knowing smile. 'Don't jump to any conclusions,' she warned. 'There are two major roadblocks to a personal relationship growing between us. One, he's my boss and two, I won't be in Plainview for long.'

Janet sighed. 'I forget that not everyone wants to go through life with a partner, a soulmate, a lover, like I do.'

'I want those things,' Heather objected.

'Then maybe you should work as hard to obtain them as you do on your job. See you later.'

Heather considered Janet's suggestion while sipping her juice on the way to her office. Even though she'd had a somber childhood, in rare, weak moments she pictured a home filled with a loving husband, several kids and at least one dog.

Unfortunately, the lack of a suitable parental role model made her hesitant to pursue that particular dream. Her fear that she'd create another generation of cold, unfeeling people might be irrational, but it still infected her. So why did Aaron and his son reawaken those desires after she'd suppressed them so success-fully for so long?

She flicked the light switch and tossed her briefcase on to the neatly arranged desk. If only Aaron Spence worked in another area of the hospital.

If he had any sense, he'd wish Heather Manning had chosen another field of medicine, Aaron thought as he overheard her discussing a case with a histology tech-nician. But he was intelligent enough to know that if that had been the case he would probably never have met her. And that was a frightening idea.

He rubbed his gritty eyes. Sleep hadn't come easily

last night. Heather, with her soft skin and responsive lips, had invaded his dreams as well as his life. At one point he'd even thought he'd smelled her floral perfume next to him in bed, and his body had reacted accordingly. But as the night wore on it had been difficult to still the voice that taunted him with dire consequences for his weak moment. In self-defense, and tired from tossing and turning, he'd stolen into his study and immersed himself in a pile of dusty journals. He'd given up reading only when his mind had become too muddled to recall a single word.

Unfortunately, he needed all his wits about him today. Voicing his concerns about Emily's job performance to Heather would be difficult in the best of circumstances; it was hard to guess how she'd receive his opinion if she felt he'd overstepped the bounds last night. Taking a silent breath, he knew her attitude this morning would dictate the path of their relationship. He prayed that she'd allow for more than just a professional association.

Heather turned and he stiffened, waiting for her reaction. Her mouth relaxed into a gentle smile and he felt as if his prayer had been answered as swiftly as it had been offered. He wanted to shout for joy, but settled for a face-splitting grin.

She crossed the room to his side. 'How about some coffee? I hear someone brought treats today. Your favorite, I hear.'

'Cinnamon rolls?'

She nodded.

He bent close to her ear. 'Who made the coffee?'

'Don't worry,' she whispered. 'It wasn't Emily. You still don't think she'd sneak something into——?'

'No.'

'Then why did you ask?'

Aaron grinned. 'Because you get this cute little wrinkle between your eyes when you're defending someone.'

'I do not.'

He held up his hands. 'No kidding.'

'Dr Spence?' Emily interrupted. 'Dr Carter called. He's on his way to see you.'

'I don't suppose I have time for my snack, do I?' He hoped so, already savoring the smell of freshly baked bread and cinnamon.

'Sorry, but since he's coming down the hall now I doubt it,' Heather said. 'I'll do my good deed for the day and save the biggest one for you.'

'Promise?'

She crossed her heart with her right index finger. 'Promise.' She disappeared in one direction while Aaron stood frozen on the spot. He imagined his own fingertip tracing the same lines over her breast. Preferably without interference from any clothing, however wispy it might be.

'Aaron,' Dr Carter greeted him. 'How are things going?'

The pathologist quickly pulled his imagination away from his colleague's feminine attributes. 'Fine,' he replied, reasonably certain that the chief of staff wasn't interested in his as yet undiscussed secretarial problems. He stretched out his arm toward his office. 'What can I do for you today?'

'Actually, it's something I'm doing for you,' Carter announced, entering the room and moving toward a vacant chair beside Aaron's desk. 'I'd like you to chair our Disaster Planning Committee. Since you've been involved in that type of work in the armed services, you're perfect for the job.'

'You surely have other physicians to handle the task?'

'I'd prefer you.' The rotund physician crossed his arms over his paunch.

'Please, don't misunderstand. I'd consider it an honor, but I'm not familiar enough with your procedures to do the job justice.'

'All the more reason you should do it. Your experience in dealing with catastrophes, coupled with your objectivity as a new physician, would allow you to detect problem areas no one else has.'

'I suppose so,' Aaron mused. 'Although I'd prefer to wait another six months or so.'

'Nonsense. The best way to learn is to jump right in.'

And drown, Aaron thought. 'All right.'

Paul slapped his hands on his thighs. 'Now that we've decided that, if you'll call Heather in, I'll break the news to her.'

'*Heather* is the chairman?' A sick feeling hit his stomach.

'Was,' Carter corrected him.

Aaron grabbed the receiver, punched a few buttons and gave a terse message to Emily requesting Heather's presence.

'I really don't think it's wise to replace her,' he began after he hung up, dreading the sticky situation about to unfold. His pencil made dull thuds as he tapped it against a notepad.

Carter waved his hand. 'This is in the best interests of the hospital and she'll understand that. But if you're worried about creating hard feelings, assign something else to her.'

Heather hesitated on the threshold, her fresh snow-white lab coat buttoned to her neck as if it served as armor. From experience, she'd suspected that she'd need something to withstand whatever news Paul Carter brought. The frown on Aaron's face definitely didn't bode well. She knocked briskly on the door while fingering her necklace with her other hand. 'You wanted to see me?'

'Have a seat, Dr Manning,' Carter boomed. 'Aaron and I were just discussing the Disaster Committee.'

'Really?' She sat down, crossed her legs and clasped her hands together in her lap.

'Aaron has agreed to serve as chairman,' Carter said.

The smile she wore froze into place. 'I see.'

'You've wanted to relinquish that job for quite a while, if memory serves me correctly,' Carter continued. 'Too time-consuming, I believe you've said.'

'Yes, but. . .' She couldn't admit that the double workload she'd carried for all those years had prompted her request.

Carter held up his hand to stop her protests. 'You've done an excellent job, but Dr Spence's experience will give us some new insight and you'll get a much needed break.' He beamed at her, as if pleased by his thoughtfulness.

More like a push out the door, Heather mused, anger rising above her hurt. 'I'll hand over my files right away,' she said stiffly, refusing to meet Aaron's gaze.

Carter nodded, rising out of his chair. 'I'll send memos to the other committee members. Aaron, I'd like to hear your comments in, shall we say, thirty days? That should give you ample time to take over the reins from Dr Manning.'

'Of course,' Aaron replied.

'Let me know if there's anything else I can do,' Carter mentioned before leaving the room.

You've done enough already, Heather silently shouted. 'I'll get those files.' Before Aaron could say another word, she too left the office.

With sure strides and her jacket crackling with every movement, she crossed the hallway and yanked open her filing cabinet. A strong sense of déjà vu came over her. What else would she lose?

Her fingers tugged on the thick file folder and she grasped it with both hands to pull it free from the packed drawer. The slam echoed behind her as she stomped back to Aaron's office and tossed the packet on his desk. It landed with a dull thud.

'Here's all the information you'll need. Have fun.' She turned on her heel as sharply as a soldier on parade. His voice stopped her before she reached the door.

'Heather, for what it's worth, I'm sorry.'

She pivoted to face him. 'I wish I could believe you.'

'I didn't know it was your project.'

'Hah!'

'I didn't,' he insisted. 'I thought the chairmanship was vacant.'

'Well, it wasn't.'

'I know that. Now.'

'You could have turned him down, you know.' She crossed her arms.

'He's my boss too. And he wants a report in a month's time.'

'Then you'd better start reading,' she retorted.

'I'd like to discuss the committee's plans with you tonight.'

'I'm busy.'

'How about tomorrow night?'

'I'm busy then too.' His raised eyebrows suggested that he had doubts about her suddenly active social life, but she didn't care.

He ran one hand through his hair. 'Look, I know this isn't a pleasant situation for you, and I truly am sorry.' His voice turned hard. 'But the fact remains that both of us have to comply with Carter's wishes. More specifically, I have a report due in thirty days—a report that I *will* make with *your* help, one way or another. Don't make me pull rank, because I'd be more than happy to accommodate.' His tone softened. 'I need you, Heather.'

She froze, startled as much by his final statement as by the initial news.

'I need you, Heather.'

The sincerity she heard created a ridiculous urge to weep. She'd waited so long, nearly an entire lifetime, to have someone tell her that. Her father, her medical school instructors, her nannies and housekeepers had always voiced what they *wanted* from her for one reason or another.

'I need you'.

Even the man she'd developed a fondness for in med school hadn't said that. For a crazy second, she wished Aaron's simple comment carried a more personal connotation.

'I need you'.

Of course he needed her, she scoffed silently. She

was the component necessary for him to slide smoothly along the paths she'd already oiled with her own hard effort. Unfortunately, her choices were extremely limited. If she refused, he could accuse her of insubordination, but agreeing seemed almost too bitter a pill to swallow.

'All right.' She sounded weary to her own ears. 'I'll cooperate, but only under protest. And I really do have plans for the next couple of evenings.'

'How about Saturday?'

She thought a moment. 'Saturday's fine,' she said quietly before slipping out of the room and heading for the elevators. She might be forced into helping him, but she didn't have to like it, she thought, stabbing the 'UP' button with her index finger.

The doors whooshed open and she stepped inside for a quick trip to the second floor. Hopefully, dealing with other people's problems would take her mind off her own.

Heather first met with Harriet Marshall, a forty-nine-year-old woman surrounded by her husband and two daughters. She left soon after seeing that Mrs Marshall had plenty of moral support and a good mental attitude for her upcoming surgery.

The second biopsy candidate, Allison Vale, was in her early twenties and visibly anxious about the process. Heather took more time with her since the girl admitted she was alone.

'I won't let them do anything major,' Allison insisted. 'If it's cancerous, I want a second opinion.'

'Getting another opinion is a good idea,' Heather agreed. 'But timeliness is important too.'

'I don't care. I want to have a husband and children some day and I don't want to be a freak.'

Heather wondered if Allison realized her very life was at stake and consequently her dreams might never materialize. Allison's attitude and the stubborn tilt of her chin kept her from mentioning that reconstructive surgery and prosthetic devices were available to take care of outward appearances. With any luck, her personal physician wouldn't need to discuss those options at all.

Leaving Allison's room, she located her third and final patient on the fifth floor.

'Good afternoon, Mrs Reddig.' She greeted the middle-aged lady and eyed the half-empty dishes. 'How was lunch?'

'Fine, but I just wasn't very hungry,' the frail woman replied from her semi-upright position. A unit of blood hung from the transfusion stand and dripped slowly into the IV tubing inserted in the woman's forearm.

'Dr Franklin told me that you had figured out I needed special blood.' Mrs Reddig talked with effort and Heather planned to keep the conversation short.

'Actually, it was a joint effort between Dr Franklin, myself and my staff.'

'I still don't understand all this talk of anti-whatevers.'

Smiling, Heather moved closer to the bed. 'It is rather confusing, but maybe I can explain it without giving an immunology lecture. Your body's natural defenses watch for foreign proteins like bacteria, blood cells or pollen. When it finds them, you then produce antibodies, or special proteins that attack and destroy whatever doesn't belong. In your case, your defense system went a little haywire. It saw something on your own red blood cells that it didn't recognize. Consequently, you developed antibodies that destroyed your own cells, making you anemic.'

'And tired,' Mrs Reddig added, brushing a lock of limp salt-and-pepper hair off her forehead.

Heather nodded. 'So to raise your hemoglobin we had to find blood that your body would think was your own. And we did.' She waved at the IV bag.

'All this trouble because of a cough,' Mrs Reddig grumbled. 'I wanted to enjoy my summer and now just look at me, wasting away in a hospital bed.'

'You have a serious lung infection and Dr Franklin is working hard to clear it up. We want you healthy, too.'

'I know, dearie,' the woman replied. 'But will I always need a blood transfusion?'

'It probably won't be necessary after your infection disappears. We will monitor your blood work for several months, though, to be sure everything returns to normal.' Heather laid her hand over Mrs Reddig's open palm and squeezed ever so gently. 'I'll let you rest. But if you have any questions, just tell one of the nurses. They'll get in touch with me.'

Mrs Reddig nodded, then closed her eyes.

Heather returned to the lab and learned that Mrs Marshall and Allison Vale were on their way into surgery. A short time later the specimens arrived and she made her diagnoses. Both growths were malignant.

And, unluckily for Allison, the lymph nodes showed traces of cancerous cells, indicating that in addition to a mastectomy she'd need intensive chemotherapy.

As much as Heather enjoyed interacting with the patients, this was one of those times she was glad she'd chosen pathology instead of family practice medicine. Bearing bad news to her medical-school patients had been her major weakness. Time after time, in spite of her resolve to remain objective, she'd empathized with the sick and dying so closely that their emotional pain had become hers.

'You can't afford to be soft-hearted', she remembered Aaron saying.

He'd never know how close his casual comment had struck home. She knew she had to remain emotionally detached from her patients, and for the most part she succeeded. But there were enough instances where she found it nearly impossible to do so. Afraid that she'd eventually become an ineffective physician, she'd decided, much to her father's joy, to follow in his footsteps. It was relatively easy in her branch of medicine to maintain an aloof objectivity.

And yet Heather couldn't help but wonder how she would deal with Allison Vale if she were the girl's personal physician. . . .

By the end of the day, Heather was exhausted. She'd worked at a frenetic pace all afternoon to keep from dwelling on the morning's discouragement. All she wanted now was to slip out the door without seeing Aaron.

He approached her desk just as she opened her briefcase and shoved a sheaf of papers inside. 'Working above and beyond the call of duty again, I see.'

'Not really,' she replied, her voice cool.

'If you're not getting everything done during the day, maybe we should consider making some changes,' he began.

Instinctively she knew what he'd say next. 'I work evenings because I *choose* to, not because I *have* to. I will *not* give up my hospital rounds.' She squared her shoulders and stared at him, unflinching under his gaze. He'd have a royal fight on his hands if he tried to take that away too.

'Actually, I came here to discuss Emily, not your work habits, although that topic may come up again.'

'Oh.' She snapped her briefcase closed.

Aaron quirked one dark eyebrow. 'Emily's job performance isn't up to standard.'

She sighed. 'I'll have a talk with her.'

'I'm afraid it's beyond that, Heather. She's making horrible mistakes. Her reports are a week behind and when I finally get them they're either full of typographical or transcription errors.

'Look at this.' He brandished a page under Heather's nose, his ire evident. 'This girl had a Class I—a normal—pap smear. I remember because Kim questioned me about some of the cells. But you can't tell it from the report because it looks like it reads Class III, with a smudge over two of the numbers. The physician seeing this wouldn't have a clue as to what, if anything, he should do for his patient.'

'She's under a lot of stress. Her workload has practically doubled since you've arrived,' she reminded him.

'Be that as it may, I won't let this continue. How can we convince the medical staff that we're professionals, that we're not running a slipshod organization, if our reports look as if a bunch of elementary-school kids typed them?'

'I understand.' But understanding didn't make Heather feel better.

'You've obviously had similar problems in the past,' he stated, crossing his arms over his chest. 'What did you do?'

'I simply asked her to retype them.'

'She needs to consider working someplace else.'

Heather was aghast. 'We can't *fire* her. She needs this job to support her family. Her husband is an alcoholic and is usually unemployed.'

'I'm sorry to hear that, but we aren't a social service agency. If she can't handle this job, she has to find one that she can, whether it's in the lab or another department.'

'We still can't fire her.'

'Don't take it personally, Heather. I know she's your friend and I know you hired her. It's hard to admit you may have misjudged her abilities.'

'I didn't misjudge her abilities. She can do the work,' she insisted.

He held up his hands. 'I won't argue the point. All I know is that she's making far too many mistakes to suit me and creating more delays. Maybe the warning I gave will help her get her act together.'

'You've already talked to her?' Poor Emily, she thought.

'I had to. I wanted these reports retyped before I'd sign them.'

'I still think I'll talk to her,' she mused aloud. 'If she wants to move into another position, I won't hold her back. On the other hand, maybe you should consider hiring more clerical staff, at least on a part-time basis.'

He shook his head. 'I've had secretaries handle twice as much work with half as many errors. Extra help isn't the answer.'

'But——'

Aaron shook his head. 'I'm telling you what I told her. One more major mistake and she won't be here to make any more. I have to consider the needs of the entire department, not just Emily's.'

A few seconds of silence passed. His cold blue eyes, flared nostrils and warning tone made it obvious that he meant every word and would overrule any objections. Feeling utterly powerless, Heather grabbed her briefcase and purse. Stalking to the door, she turned toward him. Speaking more calmly than she would have dreamed possible in the circumstances, she said, 'You're the boss.'

Doors shook behind her and her hands trembled as she steered her car toward home. Once there, she immediately gobbled a few antacids and downed a glass of milk.

Why was she attracted to a man who, like her father, seemed to have no compassion for others? she thought, stripping off her clothes and changing into her Lycra exercise outfit.

She vocalized her dismay to Janet on the way to their first aerobics class at the city gymnasium.

'If you're comparing him to your dad, you're way off base, Heather,' Janet said after listening to Heather's colorful speech on the day's events. 'I don't believe Aaron is as hard-hearted as you're painting him.'

Heather fell silent. Aaron hadn't scoffed at her hobby; he enjoyed plants and loved his son. Those points alone made him different from her parent. 'Maybe not,' she conceded halfheartedly.

'So how would you handle the problems with Emily?' Janet asked.

Heather stared at the passing scenery, reminiscing about those earlier days. She remembered feeling aggravated at the secretary's less than letter-perfect reports and the little chats when she'd emphasized the importance of quality, not quantity.

'OK, so he has a legitimate complaint,' she admitted. 'But it doesn't mean Emily should be replaced like some worn-out pair of shoes.'

Janet was quiet. 'Why do I get the impression Emily isn't the main issue?'

Heather sighed. 'Because she's not. I'm angry over Carter's sneaky maneuver.'

'I think most of us will agree that Carter is a pompous, over-inflated windbag eighty-five per cent of the time. But if you were in his position wouldn't you select someone with Aaron's particular expertise to chair that committee?'

'Probably.'

'As for Emily's ineptitude, try to see it from Aaron's perspective,' Janet advised. 'I know it's hard, especially since Carter favored Aaron with one of your assignments. But deep down you know that whatever happens in your department—good or bad—reflects on Aaron.'

'I know,' Heather replied wearily.

Janet stopped the car in front of the gymnasium. 'You'd eventually have come to the same conclusions, but aren't you glad I helped you reach them a little sooner?' She grinned.

'Yeah, right.'

'And now that you have all that anxiety out of your system you'll enjoy yourself tonight.'

Heather grabbed her towel and followed Janet into the gym. 'Look at all these crazy women wanting to sweat in a hundred-degree building. I still don't know why I let you talk me into this.'

Janet led the way to a vacant spot on the floor, accepting Heather's teasing good-naturedly. 'Because you want to wow everyone when you wear that little red dress from Maybelle's Boutique to the hospital benefit in a few weeks, that's why.'

CHAPTER SIX

WHEN God handed out compassion, you stood in line twice, Heather chided herself Saturday evening as she dried the last dish. With another swipe of the towel for good measure, she slid the plate on top of the others and closed the cupboard door.

The sounds of Aaron's deep voice and Josh's higher-pitched one drifted through the open kitchen window as they tended her herb garden. Two days ago, after surrendering to the inevitable, she'd figured she'd drop by Aaron's house, spend a few hours discussing the Disaster Committee's accomplishments and goals, then pass the reins of responsibility over to him.

But lately her plans had had a disturbing habit of changing without notice.

Aaron had called around noon to tell her they'd either have to postpone their meeting or change its location because of unexpected problems with his home-improvement project.

Postponement had been out of the question—she'd wanted this unfortunate mess behind her—and she'd known they wouldn't accomplish much at a noisy restaurant. His obvious distress, coupled with her empathy for his situation, had created a weak moment in which she'd volunteered her own quarters. After guessing they'd lived on a fast-foot diet for several days, pity for Josh had had her tack on the supper invitation.

She'd planned to maintain the aloof demeanor she'd

101

established after their argument, but watching Aaron limp across the room had chipped away chunks of her resolve. Sharing a meal had made it even more difficult to stick to her plan; she simply couldn't treat the man coldheartedly in front of his own son.

No, the mood had been too relaxed and too light-hearted for her to keep up her guard. From the moment Aaron had passed the spaghetti, it had seemed as if her dream of a family had come true.

A smile touched the corners of her mouth. And what meal wasn't complete without some sort of accidental spill? She'd waited for Aaron's outburst, chiding Josh for his clumsiness, but it never came. Instead, he'd simply helped her mop up the milk running across the table and joked, 'You're slipping, Josh. You missed me this time.'

She wiped the countertop once more, aware that her feelings for Aaron were treading dangerous waters. After their homey dinner, she'd needed time alone to get her thoughts in order. Consequently she'd brushed aside his offer to do the dishes, sending him outdoors to help Joshua with their self-appointed task.

'We're finished,' Aaron announced, coming inside with Josh at his heels.

'So am I.'

A horn sounded, sending the preteen to the front door. 'Thanks for supper, Heather. See ya after the ball game.'

'Stay with Kevin's family. No running around,' Aaron cautioned.

'I won't, Dad.' The door bounced once before it closed on its own.

Aaron moved aside a sheer curtain to peer through

the kitchen window. 'Do you think they'll cancel the game? It looks like it could get nasty outside.'

Heather joined him to study the dark blue clouds rolling across the northwestern sky. The distinctive smell of rain drifted in on the gentle breeze. 'It's hard to say. The weatherman predicted the storm would go around us, but he's been wrong before. In any case, Janet and Dave will look after the kids.'

Apparently reassured, Aaron gave up his post to retrieve his briefcase from the living room. He set it on the table.

'How's your knee?' she asked. 'I doubt if weeding is part of your prescribed treatment.'

'Josh worked while I supervised. Didn't bend down once.'

'I'm not convinced,' she said drily, seeing his nearly imperceptible grimace as he shifted his weight. 'Don't you have any pain pills?'

He nodded. 'I only take them as a last resort.'

'And when is that?' She crossed her arms.

'For your information, Dr Nosy,' he said, acting affronted, 'I broke down and took one a few minutes ago. I'm waiting for it to kick in and do its job. Besides, digging in your dirt was the least we could do in exchange for supper. I certainly wasn't expecting an invitation when I called earlier.'

'You sounded rather desperate.'

'More like furious. I still can't believe someone at the store cut the carpeting to the wrong size.'

'Mistakes do happen,' she reminded him pointedly, hoping this experience might be a lesson to him.

'I realize that. It wouldn't have been so bad if they'd found their error before they ripped out the old stuff.

But when your house is in shambles, your furniture piled into every available nook and cranny so you can't even find your way to the bathroom, it's hard to be forgiving.'

He pulled out the same oak chair he'd used at supper and sat down. With his briefcase before him, he paused with his thumbs on the locks. 'Can I ask you something before we begin?'

'Sure.'

'I've noticed how much you like to deal with patients. I'm curious as to why you chose pathology over a more people-oriented specialty.'

Heather sank into the seat on his right—Josh's chair. 'I got too involved with people's problems. I thought it best to work in an area where I couldn't do that.'

'Do you regret your decision?' he asked.

She shook her head. 'No. I like what I do.'

As if her response met with his approval, he popped open the latches and became businesslike. 'I read the old disaster plan last night and I've made some notes. They should be right here. . .' He shuffled several papers.

Their fingers touched when he handed her the page. Like before, she felt her skin tingle. Conscious movement ceased, as if neither wanted the brief contact to end. His eyes gleamed with something resembling hunger and she knew he saw the same need shining in her own.

He's your boss, a little voice taunted.

Slowly, achingly, she pulled her hand away. As much as she wanted—no, craved—his touch, she couldn't relinquish control. Getting personally involved would compound her problems and she had plenty of those already. Think cool and aloof. Think of Emily. Think of everything he's taken from you.

Regret flashed across his face before he masked it. Clearing his throat, he said, 'This document appears to have the bases covered, but I noticed a few things lacking in the areas of security, power and water.'

'Maintenance men will supplement our security staff by directing traffic and keeping the Press and sightseers away. It's outlined right here.' Heather flipped to the right page and pointed to the appropriate paragraph.

'Who will keep the hospital's equipment operational if they're busy guarding doors?'

'The maintenance men. . .' Her voice trailed away. 'I see what you mean.'

'Rather than issue a blanket policy for all the individuals in that department, we could designate a select group of them—those whose daily job isn't closely tied to the physical operation of the hospital—to function as temporary security guards. What do you think?'

She held up both hands. 'Hey, I'm not on this committee; you'll have to get someone else's opinion.'

He arched one dark eyebrow. She could see the muscles tense around his mouth and hear the steady tap of his pen against the table. 'I have a report due in thirty days—a report that I *will* make with *your* help, one way or another,' flashed through her mind, and she knew she'd blundered. Antagonizing her superior wasn't a wise move. Hoping to defuse the situation, she added hastily, 'But as an interested bystander I think your idea sounds fine. Maybe the supervisor has already addressed that issue in the department's plan.'

The lines around his mouth relaxed, the tapping noise ceased, and she felt her own tension disappear.

'Then we need to include it in ours so everyone is aware of the exact policy.' His pen scratched, leaving a barely legible sentence to dry on a fresh piece of paper.

He turned a page. 'The next topic is power. I know you have an emergency generator, but what about your backup systems?'

'We have one unit, but it can only supply electricity for the critical areas of the hospital like ICU, Surgery, and the nursery. Other areas, like ours, will be out of business if the first generator goes out.'

'Not good enough. In a disaster, you can't plan on *anything* working when you want it and no one can run to the hardware store for spare parts. Without power, we might as well hand out Band-Aids because that's all the good we'll do.'

'I realize that, but I couldn't convince Carter. Maybe you'll have more success.' Heather folded her arms across her chest. She'd pointed out the same problem a year ago, and failed to persuade the administration to spend the extra money on equipment that they probably and hopefully would never use.

The corners of Aaron's mouth inched upward and his face wore a we'll-see-about-that look. She didn't doubt for a second that he'd have any difficulties in obtaining what he thought Plainview needed. He was, after all, Carter's golden boy, his *pièce de résistance*.

'That brings us to water,' he said.

A vivid picture of Aaron in the shower, with water dripping off his dark hair and on to his bare chest, popped into Heather's head. She visualized his biceps, remembering how they'd felt when she'd run her palms up his arms. Her knees wobbled, making her glad she was sitting down. *That* was power, she thought, fidgeting in her chair. If it could be harnessed, they wouldn't need to worry about generating electricity from a collection of mechanical parts.

'Heather?' he asked. 'Are you with me?'

She forced her attention away from her fantasy and on to the present. 'Yeah. You're talking about water.'

'I didn't see where the hospital has a plan for an alternate source of water. We can't depend on the city's supply if we experience a natural disaster.'

'So we drill our own water well, or truck it here from another place,' she mused.

He agreed. 'I'll present those options in my report. The board of directors can choose which route they want to take.' Tossing the papers into his briefcase, he snapped the lid closed, then stood up and stretched.

'Are we finished?' she asked, rather surprised. She'd expected more than a few measly questions.

'For now.'

'For now?' she repeated.

He smiled at her dumbfounded look and held out his hand. 'For now. I haven't read your entire file yet, so I'm sure we'll have to meet again. But now I'm prescribing something else.' He tugged her to her feet.

With their fingers intertwined, Heather felt her heart rate speed up, fully cognizant that a very forceful man stood beside her. 'What?'

'This.' He placed his arms around hers, pinning her to his body. He lowered his head, and his mouth latched on to hers with the accuracy and precision of a surgeon performing a heart catheterization.

His warm lips demanded a response—a response she freely gave. A long sigh of pleasure worked its way through her teeth as she savored each nibble, each twist of his mouth. His heart pounded beneath her palms and she felt the rise and fall of his chest at the same time she felt his breath caress her cheek. Inching her hands around to his back, she raised herself to tiptoe height.

Leaning against him and reveling in the feel of his hard body against hers, she ignored everything—the approaching storm, his position of authority, their differences. This moment in time was too enjoyable to let worldly cares and concerns intrude.

His hands rubbed circles across her spine. His arms around her felt so good, so protective, and so perfect. Peace stole over her like a warm, thick blanket and she reveled in the joy flooding her soul.

Glass shattered, breaking the magical spell. Heather, still enfolded in Aaron's embrace, glanced in that direction. The water glass she'd placed on the counter had fallen, apparently knocked over by the curtain billowing in the strengthening breeze. 'I'd better clean up the mess.'

'Later,' he commanded. Then, stroking her cheek with a butterfly touch, he murmured, 'I enjoyed that very much.'

'I did too,' she said softly.

'I'll want to kiss you again,' he said. 'In fact, right now would be a good time.' His eyes twinkled like polarized crystals and his mouth curved into a wicked grin.

With a burst of insight, she finally realized what Janet had meant by wanting a lover, a soulmate, a partner, at her side. Now that she had a taste of what could be, she wondered if any job or hobby, no matter how wonderful, could satisfy that craving.

Raindrops hit against the windows. 'I'd agree, except it's raining and the window is open,' she said.

'Then I'll allow a postponement,' he replied, dropping his arms. 'A *brief* postponement.'

Heather walked toward the sink and stepped gingerly around the glass to reach the window. She slammed it closed just as lightning streaked across the sky with thunder booming in its wake.

'I'm glad Josh is with Janet and Dave,' Aaron said as he carefully gathered the larger of the broken pieces while she rummaged in the closet for a broom.

'Why don't you turn on the radio? We might hear an updated weather bulletin.'

He disappeared into the living room while she whisked the fragmented remains into a dustpan. A few minutes later, she joined him.

Before she could ask the question hovering on her lips, he volunteered the information. 'They haven't said a word about the storm yet. I suppose the philosophy of no news is good news applies. I know Josh is with Dave, but I still can't help worrying.'

'I think that's a natural parental reaction,' she reassured him, watching him study the sky from the large window. 'I won't hold it against you.'

The telephone rang. Listening to the caller, she motioned to her guest. 'He's right here, Josh,' she told him before extending the receiver to her guest.

'What's up, son?' Aaron remained silent, then glanced at his watch. 'I'll be there no later than nine. That gives you forty-five minutes.'

'You've made someone happy, I'll bet,' she said after he replaced the receiver.

'Josh wanted to play at Kevin's house since their baseball game was canceled.'

'I'm glad they're getting along so well. Is Josh anxious about school starting in a few weeks?' she asked.

'Yes, but not as much as I'd expected. I think sharing a lot of classes with Kevin has eased his mind.'

'Does the principal know about Josh's experience?'

Aaron nodded. 'He fixed Josh's schedule to coincide with Kevin's as much as possible. He said he'd alert the teachers and keep an eye open for problems.' He rubbed the back of his neck and stared at the floor.

'With an outgoing friend like Kevin, I'm sure there won't be any,' Heather responded firmly, guessing that a sight other than her carpeting had appeared before his eyes.

In the silence that followed, she heard a distinct pitter-patter sound on the roof. 'It's raining,' she mentioned inanely. 'How about something to drink? Or eat?' she tacked on, thinking of his sweet tooth.

'Any more of those chocolate-chip cookies?' he asked hopefully, his eyes meeting hers.

'I think so.' She disappeared into the kitchen while he clicked off the radio.

The telephone jingled again. 'Could you get that, please?' she called out, arranging her homemade treats on a plate.

Aaron walked into the kitchen as she popped the tops of two soft-drink cans. 'It's for you. I can finish in here.'

Leaving him with the tray, Heather walked to the desk phone. 'Hello?'

'Who is that man, Heather?' the deep, harsh voice demanded.

'Hi, Dad.' She felt her stomach begin to tense. 'My boss, Aaron Spence, is here.'

'Socializing?'

She heard the disapproving note in his voice. Her father was as much a master at conveying his opinion without words as with them. Wondering why she always felt compelled to explain, she replied, 'No, we've been working on disaster plans.'

'Ah. They've added him to your committee, have they?'

'Not exactly. He's chairing it now.' Why did her father have to call tonight? She could have sworn he had mental radar that knew exactly when she was ill-prepared to deal with him.

'What?' Dr Manning demanded.

'He's very experienced in this sort of thing, Dad,' she explained in a low voice, aware of Aaron's presence in the other room.

'I don't understand, Heather. How could this have happened?'

'He replaced me. It's that simple,' she said flatly, already rummaging for the antacids she'd stashed in the desk for such occasions.

'Hmmph! Have you heard anything from your job inquiries?'

'I have an interview in three weeks in Oklahoma City.'

'Good heavens. That's even farther away from home than Plainview. Can't you find anything closer?'

Not if I can help it. 'Sorry,' she said, trying to sound apologetic. Seeing Aaron enter the room, she added, 'I'd love to talk longer, but I really can't. I'll call next weekend. Bye.'

Hanging up the phone, she saw that he had set the tray on the coffee table. Immediately she popped two tablets into her mouth. Twisting her necklace into a knot, she blurted, 'I'd like to take a few days off in a few weeks' time, if it's OK with you.'

'Problems?' His brow furrowed.

In a manner of speaking, she thought. 'No.' His questioning look had her adding, 'That was my dad.' She plopped on to a chair and chewed on her bottom lip. She should probably volunteer this particular information since in all likelihood he'd overheard her relay the news to her father. It wasn't as if he didn't know that she planned to leave Plainview when the opportunity arose. 'I'd planned to ask on Monday, but I may as well ask now. I have a job interview two weeks from Friday.'

She waited for his reply. He pursed his lips, as if weighing his answer. 'Ordinarily, I'd say yes. But have you forgotten the health fair starts that Monday?'

'And ends Tuesday,' she finished, prepared for that objection. 'The staff in the clinical lab have everything under control. They'll handle all the blood work and the secretaries will attach my form letter to all abnormal reports.'

'And the PSA tests?'

'Statistically, we shouldn't find that many positive results, so I can contact those patients before I leave. I only need Thursday and Friday free.' If necessary, she'd remind him that she hadn't had any time to call her own in almost a year.

He nodded slowly. 'No problem. I can surely hold the fort together for two days. When will you get back?'

'Sometime on Saturday. I'd considered flying to Oklahoma City, but decided I'd rather drive.'

'How far is it?'

'About eight hours. I thought I'd do some sightseeing, too. If the interview doesn't work out, at least my trip won't have been a total waste.'

'Think positive,' he advised.

But, driving through the rain to reclaim Josh, Aaron discovered that he didn't want to 'think positive'. Hearing that she had a prospect at another hospital had spoiled his evening, although he'd tried hard to disguise his feelings. He didn't want Heather to leave Plainview, for purely personal reasons. In fact, thoughts of marriage had been popping into his head with amazing regularity.

Luckily they'd reclaimed the rapport they'd lost, and more successfully than he'd hoped after one evening. Even though he knew he had to exercise patience, he'd wanted to declare how he felt about her. Unfortunately circumstances in addition to his own fear that she'd reject him had checked his impulse. Then again, God only knew what would have happened if her father hadn't telephoned.

His hands ached from gripping the steering wheel. He'd seen her agitation after the conversation and although she'd tried to hide it he'd seen her devour those antacids like a candy addict. Either her father was unaware of his effect on her or he knew and didn't care. Grimacing in disgust at a man he'd never seen, he wished for an opportunity to meet him face to face. Handicapped or not, the elder Dr Manning deserved a punch on the nose—and he'd love to be the man to inflict it.

* * *

'I thought you said everything was under control,' Aaron muttered to Heather as they weaved through the crowd spilling out of the lab's waiting room into the hallway.

'It was,' she replied, following him into his office and taking a seat. 'The two girls who were assigned to draw blood aren't here. One has the flu and the other had a death in the family over the weekend. Since we didn't have anyone else to spare, the regular specimen-collection staff are working the health fair participants in with our usual patients.' She grinned. 'Be grateful the fair only lasts for two days and not the entire week.'

'I suppose. By the way, did you see the medical release on Allison Vale? She wants her reports to go to a specialist at the Kansas University Medical Center.'

'She told me when I saw her that she planned to get a second opinion. I don't blame her. I did the same thing.'

'Oh, really?' His eyes widened.

His interest was obvious, and Heather realized she'd divulged something that no one, other than Janet, knew about. It wasn't a secret; she'd just never felt the need to discuss it.

'I discovered a tumor right before I graduated from med school. It scared me to death, but I was lucky. The growth was malignant, but well enough defined that the surgeon was positive he'd removed it all without performing a mastectomy. I wanted another opinion to be certain more surgery wasn't necessary.' She paused. 'As happy as I was with the treatment, I didn't want to take any chances.'

'What did your father think?'

'I didn't tell him.'

'Why not?' He sounded as puzzled as he looked.

'He was frustrated with his own physical limitations at the time and I thought it best not to worry him.' She'd given the same excuse to her surgeon and to everyone else who'd asked. No one needed to know the real reason—that she'd been afraid of her father's reaction. If he'd treated her with his usual lack of moral support and concern for her feelings, she knew she wouldn't have survived her emotional roller-coaster ride.

'So you suffered alone.'

Heather looked away under his steady gaze. 'No. I had a girlfriend—a fellow classmate—who was there for me.'

'I'm glad,' he said, sounding sincere. 'So, will you see that Emily sends out Ms Vale's report as soon as possible, or shall I?'

'I'll remind her,' she promised.

'Good. I saw this morning's results on Caitlin Burns. They haven't changed since we began monitoring her.'

'I know. With nothing to fight off a bacterial infection, I'd expect her to be sick with one thing or another. But she seems so healthy.' She shook her head. 'I don't understand it.'

'We can't explain everything,' he reminded her. 'But I think it's time you recommended a bone marrow.'

'I don't know,' she said slowly. 'It's only been a few weeks.'

'A few weeks with no change,' he reminded her. 'We need to see what's going on. We've waited in the dark long enough, and I'm sure her parents would agree. Delaying isn't giving them peace of mind.'

'Maybe not, but I still think we should postpone the

procedure for a while. You know as well as I that some viruses are harder to fight than others.' Heather spoke directly, defending her position.

After a brief pause, he nodded. 'I'll give you ten days. No more.'

'Ten days? That's all?'

'Ten days,' he repeated firmly. 'Take it or leave it.'

'I'll take it,' she said wearily.

'Excuse me, Doctors,' Emily interrupted from the doorway. 'We have a gentleman outside who'd like to talk to one of you about the PSA test.'

Heather looked at Aaron. He waved his hand in a be-my-guest manner. Turning toward Emily, she said, 'Show him into my office, Em.'

A few minutes later, the secretary introduced Milton Evers, a short, stocky, middle-aged man wearing faded jeans and a khaki shirt obviously suited for outdoor work.

'Please have a seat, Mr Evers,' Heather said, sinking into her own chair. 'I understand you'd like to talk about the PSA test.'

'Yeah. I want to know how accurate it is.' The man twisted his cap in his hands.

'It's very accurate, and that's why it's used as a screening test. It often detects problems before they'd be noticeable otherwise.'

'My family has a history of prostate cancer. I haven't felt any lumps, but. . .'

'I think it's wise you're checking yourself, Mr Evers, and it's also smart that you're requesting this blood test. Have you talked to your regular physician?'

He shook his balding head. 'Not yet. I didn't see the need.'

Heather leaned forward. 'Maybe not, but it wouldn't hurt to visit with him. With your history, I'm sure he'd give you a very thorough exam.'

He looked thoughtful. 'I just don't want him to think I'm paranoid about this.'

'Concern about your body isn't paranoia, it's good sense. We'll send a copy of these results to you and your doctor. If the test detects any abnormalities, I'll also telephone you in the next day or two. So don't worry, Mr Evers.'

The gentleman got to his feet. Walking toward the door, he spoke. 'You think I should make an appointment now?'

'Have you had a recent physical?' she asked, already suspecting his answer as she skirted her desk to follow him.

He shook his head.

'You might consider scheduling a visit. Even if your test is negative, you can use that time to discuss your history and get a complete check-up. Your physician can then answer more specific questions for you.'

'OK. Thanks, Dr Manning.' He shook her hand.

'You're welcome. I'll be in touch.'

The man left the room with purpose in his step. Heather felt certain that her pep talk had encouraged him to see his primary health care provider if for no other reason than to obtain a physical.

The warm glow she felt inside carried her through most of the day, although she knew that a good part of that was anticipation of her working mini-vacation.

But by Wednesday anticipation was also laced with nervousness. She knew, without benefit of her father's reminders, how important her upcoming interview was to her career. Luckily, work occupied nearly every moment, keeping her too busy to spend time on worry. There would be plenty of time for that during the drive south to Oklahoma.

The chemistry lab supervisor cornered her in the hallway immediately after lunch. 'Dr Manning? We have a small problem.'

'What's that, Maggie?'

'I mentioned the other day that the extra reagents for the PSA tests hadn't arrived yet and I was hoarding what we had left.' While Heather nodded, remembering the brief conversation, Maggie continued. 'One of the lab aides accidentally knocked over the kit and spilled our last bottle.'

Heather shook her head, feeling both disappointed and disgusted. She'd wanted to call Mr Evers as soon as possible. 'Let me guess. Hilary?'

Maggie's grin was lopsided and she nodded as she spoke. 'I've already called the vendor. They say they shipped our order, and claim we should have received it by now. They've put out a tracer to find it, but even if I got those supplies today I wouldn't be able to finish the tests before you leave.'

'When do you think you'll have them?'

Maggie shrugged. 'Friday, I hope.'

Heather thought a moment. 'OK. Have the secretaries send out the results like we agreed, and I'll follow up with phone calls on Monday. I'd prefer to call those people before they receive their reports, but it can't be helped.'

She walked into her office, calling over her shoulder with an afterthought. 'Oh, and Maggie? Would you tell

Dr Spence the situation in case he has to deal with an irate customer?'

Dismay flooded Maggie's face. 'OK,' she sighed. 'If you insist.'

'Sending Daniel into the lion's den, I see,' Kim remarked on Heather's heels.

'What?' Heather swung round to face the cytotech.

Kim thumbed in Maggie's direction. 'Maggie and Dr Spence.'

'I saw she didn't seem too happy, but I thought she was just apprehensive about confessing there'd been a screw-up.'

'I'm sure that's part of it, but Dr Spence isn't in a good mood, you know. He hasn't been all week.'

'Oh, really?' Heather sat down and eyed the stacks of forms waiting for her attention. Busy with her own agenda, she'd hardly seen or spoken to him for several days now.

'Yeah. He's not a happy cowboy.'

Heather dismissed Kim's comments. 'He has a lot on his mind this week. Remodeling problems, Josh starting school, his knee is probably giving him fits, and he'll be on his own for a few days while I'm gone. I'm sure that's all it is.'

'Then I'll pray next week is better,' Kim replied drily. 'Enjoy yourself while you're gone, knowing that we're suffering without you.'

'I'll do my best.' Heather grinned, wondering if the inherent stress of an interview could be classified in the realm of having a good time.

Kim's voice changed to a whisper. 'Good luck, too.'

'Thanks. I'll need it,' Heather whispered back. She'd told only a few people besides Aaron, namely Janet and Kim, her true reason for leaving town. Speculation and rumors would fly soon enough if her trip was a success, she thought as she immersed herself in reports.

An hour later, just after she'd dotted the last i, Aaron breezed through the doorway. 'I thought you'd be leaving soon, so I came to wish you good luck.'

'Thanks.'

'Nervous?'

'A little,' she admitted. 'Are you?'

Aaron looked blank, then he smiled as understanding dawned. He repeated her answer. 'A little.' He sat down and stretched out his legs.

'You'll be fine,' she encouraged.

'That's my line,' he protested with a smile.

Heather grinned. 'You have good people to work with so go easy on them.'

'Aha. Word *has* spread that Dr Spence is on the warpath.'

She laughed. 'Nothing so melodramatic. Everyone's entitled to a bad week, and this one's yours. In a few days it will all be behind you.'

'I could say the same for you.' His grin disappeared.

She nodded. Although he'd been referring to her upcoming interview, it struck her that his comment could also apply to her time at Plainview. She wasn't sure if she liked the idea of having her life in this small community condensed into a few sentences on a curriculum vitae. Her smile dimmed.

As if he'd read her mind, he asked, 'Are you certain this is what you want to do?'

CHAPTER SEVEN

HEATHER toyed with her locket. Logically, her answer was an unequivocal yes. She'd worked hard and both she and her father had dreamed of the day she'd reach the top of her career ladder. And yet. . .

'Of course I am,' she answered.

'You're frowning,' Aaron remarked.

Feeling his scrutiny, she called up a weak smile. 'I was just trying to remember all my last-minute errands,' she fibbed. She reminded herself that everyone had jitters when the time came to make changes in his or her life. The nervous twitch in her stomach was simply a normal reaction.

He nodded, his face showing no sign that he doubted her word. 'Is there anything Josh or I can do while you're gone? Pick up your mail, water the plants, or feed the fish?'

'Actually,' she began tentatively, 'I'd planned to ask Kevin if he'd get my newspaper and water my plants. Maybe Josh would like to help?'

'No problem,' he said. 'When will you be back?'

'Late Saturday afternoon. I thought I'd stop in Wichita to visit an old friend from med school I haven't seen in a long time.'

'That's nice.'

Heather couldn't help but notice his flat tone. Inwardly she smiled, wondering if perhaps he was a little jealous. She decided to wait until she returned to explain that her fellow student was a gorgeous redhead named Susan.

He rose to his feet. 'Are there any cases I should know about before you leave?'

She chewed on her bottom lip as she mentally reviewed the surgery schedule. 'There's a liver biopsy tomorrow, but everything else is fairly routine. I've signed the last of my reports and consultations, and I'll follow up the health fair participants on Monday. Unless you, of course, need something to occupy your spare time.' She grinned.

'I doubt there'll be much of that,' he said wryly.

'I'm afraid you're right.' Once again, she wondered if now was a good time to leave. Aaron had only been with them a few weeks and there were a lot of details he hadn't learned yet. 'Maybe I should cancel this appointment,' she offered. 'There'll be other openings.'

'Don't be ridiculous, Heather. Everything is planned. Besides, if I can't handle two days alone, then I don't deserve my position.' He held his hands in the air. 'Now, don't argue. Gather your things and I'll see you on Monday.'

With a two-fingered mock-salute, Heather obeyed.

'I appreciate your call, Dr Carlson, and I'm terribly sorry about the report you received. Somehow it fell through the cracks.' Aaron's jaw ached from gritting his teeth and he felt his blood pressure rise.

'I understand completely. At least now I know how I'll advise Allison Vale.' With that parting comment, the oncologist disconnected the long-distance call.

His decision made before the dial tone sounded in his ear, Aaron immediately punched four digits.

Enough was enough and in this case a solution was overdue. 'Emily? My office. Now,' he commanded.

The secretary approached the door in less than a minute with a timid knock. 'Yes, Dr Spence?' Extra wrinkles on her face testified her apprehension.

He motioned to a chair. 'Have a seat.'

She sat on the edge.

'Dr Carlson from the KU Medical Center just telephoned about a report we faxed him this morning.'

She nodded. 'Allison Vale. I remember.'

'Do you remember anything else about that report?' he asked coldly.

She shook her head, her eyes as wide as petri dishes.

Aaron refused to let her fright deter him from his purpose. He picked up a form off his desk and handed it to her. 'Read it,' he demanded.

'No malignant cells found,' she read in a quavery voice.

'Unfortunately, Ms Vale's frozen section *did* reveal a malignancy. Imagine my surprise when her specialist called about the discrepancy between her regular physician's report and ours. Not only that, but Dr Manning hasn't released this document yet. Would you care to explain?'

He crossed his arms over his chest and held his temper. Emily's mistake was inexcusable and it was doubly embarrassing that a specialist at another facility had discovered the error. He knew his clipped tone — the one his close friends called 'a knee-knocker' — was notorious for making hapless medical students and staff cower. Over the years it had proved more effective than the ranting and raving performed by some of his illustrious colleagues. Emily's blunder wasn't beyond correction, but the potential for deadly repercussions to Allison Vale made his gut twist into a hard knot. He would do whatever was necessary to ensure that errors like this wouldn't happen again.

'I'm sorry,' Emily sniffled. 'It was in the stack that Dr Manning left on my desk yesterday. I didn't see that she hadn't signed it.' She lowered her head and wiped away a tear that trickled down one cheek.

'How did you possibly make such a mistake?' He couldn't imagine how it had happened, except through gross inattention.

She kept her gaze focused on the floor.

'I want all the reports typed on that day pulled. I hope we won't find other discrepancies.' The idea that another patient might have received Ms Vale's positive report sent a fresh surge of acid into his stomach.

'Yes, sir,' she murmured. Tears trickled, then flooded down her face.

Aaron hated to deal with a weeping woman. With a great sigh, he thrust a box of tissues on to her lap.

'Am. . .am I fired?' Emily choked out, staring at him through dull, reddened eyes.

'We can't fire her.' Heather's voice echoed out of the mists of his memory.

Just watch me, he thought. Maybe he couldn't terminate her over past nuisance mistakes, but this went beyond a sloppy typographical error.

'She needs this job. . .'

Heather's face appeared before him. Damn. What a predicament! He could either compromise his principles or risk mutiny. The choice was easy to make. He was the boss and Heather would simply have to accept his decision.

'I can't trust your work,' he began gruffly. 'People's lives depend on your accuracy and I don't have the time or inclination to look over your shoulder.'

'I understand,' Emily whispered, blotting her eyes with the tissue again. 'I shouldn't have let Dr Manning talk me into this job even though it had a higher salary. But she was so certain I could do it that I really felt I could.'

Aaron wasn't surprised. He could imagine Heather giving Emily—and others—pep talks to bolster their confidence. Suddenly he wondered who held *her* up when she was down. It certainly wasn't her father.

'Dr Spence? Surgery is sending that liver biopsy now,' Kim announced from the doorway.

'I'll be right there,' he said, wishing for ten more minutes to deal with the present crisis and knowing he had none. Rising, he looked down at Emily. 'We'll finish this discussion later.'

Visibly shaken, the secretary nodded. As he strode toward the histology lab, he forced the problem into the back of his mind. This patient, as did every one, deserved his full attention.

'What's the scoop on this guy?' Kim asked, carrying the tagged specimen to the dissecting table while Aaron tied a plastic apron over his clothing.

'Theodore Trowbridge is a sixty-six-year-old man who was admitted because of mild abdominal pain, fatigue, malaise and jaundice. He has an enlarged spleen and liver, which isn't surprising considering his liver-function tests are horribly elevated.'

'Alcohol or drug abuse?'

'The patient denies it.' He pulled a pair of gloves over his hands with a snap.

'Cancer?'

'No history.'

'What about hepatitis?' Kim asked, handing him a scalpel.

'Tests for both hepatitis A and B are negative. The HIV and hepatitis C test results are pending.' He grinned. 'Sounds like alphabet soup, doesn't it? The old-timers called the first type infectious and the second type serum hepatitis. It makes me wonder how they would have described the forms we now call C and D.'

It wasn't long before Aaron placed a slide with a single layer of cellular tissue under the microscope lens. 'Bands of scar tissue, inflammatory cells and dead liver cells are present,' he dictated into his pocket tape recorder. 'Findings are consistent with liver cirrhosis.'

'What caused Trowbridge's problems if it wasn't hepatitis or drug abuse?' she asked after he'd finished.

'We haven't ruled out that disease completely,' he told her. 'He might be a hepatitis C virus carrier. Since he had a blood transfusion in the late sixties, before HIV testing was available, he may have contracted a mild case then. Less than a quarter of the carriers develop cirrhosis, but, from what I've read and the few cases I've seen, treatment with alpha interferon works well since it's a substance that inhibits viral growth.'

'But he still has a long recovery ahead of him,' Kim commented.

'I'm afraid so. He'll need his liver-function tests monitored closely for at least six months.'

Finished with his assessment, he decided to break for lunch. He'd deal with Emily after taking time out for a peaceful meal.

Thirty minutes later, fortified by steaming lasagne

and chitchat with some of his colleagues, he encountered Plainview's pediatrician.

'Aaron,' Jim Wheeler hailed him outside the cafeteria. 'I hear you're on your own for a few days.'

'Afraid so.' Aaron eyed the blond-haired pediatrician. Every time their paths crossed, it always amazed him that this man, built like a seasoned football player, chose to work with children.

'I won't keep you, but I'd like to talk a minute about a patient of mine—Caitlin Burns.'

Aaron's heart thumped faster the instant he heard the name, already anticipating Jim's conversation. 'Oh, yes, Heather and I discussed the case not long ago. What's on your mind?'

Jim explained his dilemma. By the time the two men agreed on their course of action, Aaron knew it would be very hard on Heather when she discovered the changes that had taken place during her brief absence. He could only hope that they'd still be on speaking terms by the end of the day.

'I want to hear every last detail,' Janet announced as soon as Heather swung the door open Sunday evening. 'I've been on pins and needles waiting for you to get home.'

Heather smiled. 'Well, I left on Wednesday and arrived in Oklahoma City at——'

Janet plopped on to the sofa, tucked one leg underneath her and waved her hands. 'Now quit teasing. I don't want *those* details. Just start from your interview.'

'I met the hospital administrator and the medical director, along with the two other pathologists on staff.

The lab facilities are very nice and up to date, and the people seemed very friendly.' Heather paused.

'And?' Janet prompted.

'And we had a nice visit. They explained the duties of the chief pathologist, asked me a few questions about my work at Plainview, and that was about it.'

'Are you still interested now that you've seen their set up?'

Heather fiddled with the top button of her blouse. How could she describe her thoughts when she hadn't made any sense of them yet? 'I think it would be a wonderful place to work, but. . .'

'But what?' Janet persisted.

'I don't know,' she moaned. 'I just have the idea that their chief pathologist spends his day either in meetings or pushing paper. That's OK, I guess, but it almost seems like their system is so impersonal. It's such a large hospital, they don't have time to actually see the patients, except in the morgue. It's a little late by then,' she finished drily.

Janet pursed her lips. 'Maybe you should concentrate your job-hunting efforts on smaller places like Plainview.'

'Maybe. Anyway, you've heard me mention my friend Susan?' Janet nodded and Heather continued. 'When I stopped in Wichita to visit her, she gave me another lead. A pathologist in Newton is retiring, so I contacted them.'

'What did they have to say?'

'They invited me to stop by there on my way home, which I did. The hospital is about the same size as ours and, like us, has two pathologists on staff. I think I have a good chance there too.'

'I'm glad you had a good trip,' Janet said. 'But now comes the hard part—the waiting.'

'The Oklahoma administrator said they'd make their decision next week, but the other facility isn't in any hurry. Their personnel office just placed ads in several national magazines and so it will be some time until they select a replacement.'

'It doesn't hurt to keep looking, though.'

'I suppose not. I just hate to waste the effort if one of these two places want me.'

'It is a difficult decision,' Janet admitted. 'But a few weeks, more or less, won't make that much difference.'

'So, what happened while I was gone?' Although she was interested in hospital news, Heather hoped Janet would include an update on the Spences.

'Let me see.' Janet narrowed her eyes in thought and tapped her forefinger on her lips. 'The health fair was a huge success. A record crowd showed up for the screenings.'

'That's wonderful. Is Josh worrying about school starting soon?'

'Kevin says he feels fine about it.'

'What about Aaron?'

Janet's mouth relaxed into a huge smile. 'I'm rather surprised you didn't rush to the lab as soon as you got into town,' she teased.

Heather grinned.

'You didn't!' Janet exclaimed.

'I considered it, but no, I didn't. I can't let the boss think I don't have confidence in him.'

'I'm glad you're finally learning to slow down and let someone else handle the call of duty. And don't forget that when you leave Aaron will have to manage on his own.'

Heather's subconscious replayed Janet's last sentence throughout the rest of the evening. If she accepted another position, she'd have to relinquish everything she'd established at Plainview. Would Aaron and her successor continue with her patient visits?

Aaron seemed in favor of having the physicians perform their own bone marrows. Would the policy she'd instituted fall by the wayside, forcing each physician to perform a procedure he or she might not feel comfortable doing?

And what about the health fairs? Would the lab fall back into the rut of only offering the standard cholesterol checks?

And what about all her other ideas?

Do you really want to leave? a little inner voice whispered.

Of course she did, she scolded herself. Friends and family could fail her, but she'd always have her career.

Heather walked into Emily's office the next morning and stopped short at the sight of a young brunette typing at the desk. 'Good morning, Dr Manning,' she said, before resuming her work.

Heather tried not to let her surprise show. 'Good morning,' she replied as she headed for the coffee pot on top of the dormitory-sized refrigerator. 'I should know you, but. . .' She poured herself a half-cup and dropped in an ice cube, noticing the sugar supply had been replenished.

'I'm Ruth. I used to handle the insurance billing.'

'It's good to have another secretary,' Heather said.

'Heaven knows we needed one.' She quickly downed her now lukewarm brew and left the mug next to the pot. 'I'll be in the histology lab if you need me.'

Striding down the corridor, she couldn't help the smile that spread across her face. Apparently Aaron had taken her suggestion and found someone to help Emily catch up on the paperwork that had fallen behind.

'Did you miss me?' Heather asked Kim once she arrived in the lab. She tied a white plastic apron over her navy blue scrub suit.

'Sure. You knew we would,' Kim replied, recording patient names and sample numbers into a logbook. She scooted her chair back and approached Heather. 'How was your interview?' she whispered even though they were the only two people in the room.

Heather held out her hand and wiggled it in a 'so-so' motion.

'I'll keep my fingers and toes crossed for you,' Kim responded.

'Thanks.' Switching to her normal volume, Heather asked, 'How did everything go last week? Smoothly, I hope?' She picked up a bagged specimen and carried it over to the surface where they dissected the tissues.

'We had our moments.'

Remembering Aaron's mood, Heather smiled, certain that everyone had stepped lightly around him. 'Anything serious?' Even though a tiny portion of her ego wanted to hear that they couldn't function without her, she expected Kim to report a relatively uneventful two days.

When Kim didn't reply, Heather pivoted to face the cytotech. Fear leaped into her stomach and she felt her pulse respond to the adrenalin surge. 'What happened?'

Kim grimaced, as if pained. 'Well, we had a situation that I guess you could say was both good and bad. Emily made——'

Hearing the secretary's name made Heather's heart sink like sediment in a stain bottle. No wonder she hadn't seen her familiar face in the office this morning— Ruth had replaced her. Heather tossed her scalpel on to the stainless-steel surface. Metal bounced against metal, filling the air with its recognizable clatter for a few seconds. Tearing off her latex gloves to wash her hands, she demanded, 'What did she do?'

'Do you remember an Allison Vale?'

Heather nodded. 'Positive breast biopsy. We sent the tumor to the lab in California for assays to determine what drug, if any, will be effective in treatment.'

'Well, apparently Ms Vale went to a cancer specialist in Kansas City and Emily faxed our report——'

'But I hadn't released it, yet,' Heather interrupted.

'I know. But the real problem was that Emily's report read that we didn't find a malignancy.'

'Oh, my God,' Heather moaned, pressing her fingers to her temples. Guessing the answer, she had to ask anyway. 'Who——?'

'Discovered the error? The specialist.' Heather groaned again while Kim continued, 'He called to verify the report since it didn't coincide with her other medical records.'

'And Aaron was furious.' Heather could well imagine how he'd reacted. With his previously expressed dissatisfaction over Emily's sloppy, inaccurate reports, he wouldn't give the poor girl another opportunity to redeem herself. In the circumstances, she couldn't blame him, either.

'I saw Dr Spence while he was looking up the log's entry, and I think "furious" is an understatement. But I have to give the guy credit. He handled himself very well. No one heard any yelling, screaming or glass breaking,' Kim joked. 'Hey, where are you going? There's more.'

I'm sure there is, Heather thought to herself as she stormed down the hall. Hoping to corner him in his office, she caught him just as he arrived, looking cooler and more satisfied than she felt he had a right to be.

'Good morning, Heather. How was——?'

'I want to talk to you,' she broke in, ignoring his pleasantry.

'OK.' He walked to the window and lifted some of the leaves to check the plants' soil. 'I just watered these last week. This hot weather is really drying out——'

Taking offense at his unconcerned tone and relaxed stance, she interrupted, 'Emily. I want to talk about Emily.'

'Of course. I should have known.' He walked around his desk and sat down. Leaning back in his padded chair, he steepled his fingers and held them to his mouth. 'So what's the problem?'

'What's the problem?' she repeated, hardly believing he could be so obtuse. Surely he hadn't forgotten the incident from only a few days ago? Standing with the desk between them, she leaned forward to spread her palms on the smooth surface. 'Firing Emily is the problem.'

He lowered his hands and opened his mouth, but she forestalled him with a brisk wave. 'I understand she made a terrible error, and I can't blame you. But couldn't you have worked something out instead? Firing her is so, so drastic.'

'Yes, it is.'

'Then why did you?' She straightened, moving her hands to her hips in a defiant gesture as she glared at him. His well-proportioned features made her wish this man didn't send her pulses racing, even without a confrontation.

'Who said I did?'

Her mind froze. Kim hadn't actually *said* that Emily had been dismissed. 'Emily isn't here.'

'She isn't in her office,' he corrected her.

'That's right. Ruth is.'

'And unless Emily is ill today she's probably at Ruth's old desk handling——'

'Insurance claims,' Heather finished, sinking into the chair as understanding dawned.

'Now don't you feel a little foolish for jumping to conclusions?' The smile on his face stretched from ear to ear.

She felt blood rush to her face. 'What else could I think?' she defended, certain that he'd enjoyed seeing her suspect the worst. 'You'd threatened that you wouldn't tolerate any more mistakes.'

'And I meant it.'

'Then what made you change your mind?'

He shifted position. 'I asked the office manager if she had any ideas and everything just fell into place. Emily didn't want the stress and Ruth was bored asking people how they'd pay their bill. We agreed we had nothing to lose if we let them switch jobs. Hopefully, it will avoid the hassles of vacant positions and training two new people.'

She got to her feet and Aaron followed suit, skirting the furniture to reach her side. 'Thanks, Aaron. I appreciate what you did for Emily.'

'I only provided her with another opportunity,' he said. 'Let's just hope she can handle this job better than her old one.'

Heather placed one hand on his forearm. 'Thanks, anyway.' Staring into his blue eyes, she felt his muscular strength through the cotton sleeve. She took a deep breath, inhaling a full dose of his pleasant scent, and allowed herself a small smile. It felt good to be back, even after a mere four-day absence. She'd conjured memories from her five senses during that time but they hadn't, *couldn't* compare with reality.

And right now she wanted reality. She wanted to feel his warmth surrounding her, his body molded to hers. Licking her lips, she wondered if he knew she wanted to kiss him although now wasn't the proper time or place. The challenge in his eyes indicated that he did, and that he was waiting for her to make the first move.

Before she could dissuade herself, she stood on tiptoe and brushed her mouth against his cheek before turning away. Although it wasn't a passionate encounter, it was the most she'd risk in the circumstances.

He grabbed her before she could skitter out of reach. With a light nudge of his size eleven shoe, the door closed with a quiet click. The normal sounds outside the room were muted, creating a quiet cocoon of privacy.

'Welcome back,' he whispered. He enfolded her in his arms and his mouth latched on to hers in a kiss that shook her down to her socks.

* * *

'Mr Evers?' Heather spoke into the telephone after identifying herself. 'I see your PSA test was positive and I wanted to be certain you received a copy of the results in the mail.'

'Yes, I did. I guess it was a good thing I made an appointment after I talked to you,' Milton answered.

'I'd say so.'

'Do you think it's cancer?' he asked.

'I really can't say,' she admitted, using her most reassuring voice. 'The results only indicate something is happening in your prostate that isn't considered normal. Your doctor will have to run tests to determine what that might be. Regardless, I suspect we caught whatever it is in an early stage.'

'I hope so,' he said fervently.

After breaking the connection, Heather considered the statistics of their screening program. Although they'd only encountered three abnormal test samples, she was pleased that there were three men who now had a better chance of living out their normal life span.

Leaning back, she closed her eyes and immediately relived the moment with Aaron's arms and his pleasant scent encircling her. One couldn't have asked for a more special welcome, although she did wish he'd been a little more verbal. Then again, it was foolish to talk about love and commitment when they both knew it was only a matter of time until she'd leave. She didn't need more complications than she already had.

But her logic couldn't prevent her from daydreaming a 'what if' scenario where she wasn't searching for another position and her relationship with Aaron bloomed like a desert rose.

A brisk knock at the door sent her eyelids flying open. 'Come in,' she called.

'Dr Manning? Are you handling the bone marrow this afternoon or is Dr Spence?'

Heather's eyes widened. 'I wasn't aware we had one scheduled.'

'Yeah. Dr Spence arranged it last Thursday, I believe. I assumed you'd do it, so I thought I'd ask if you wanted any special supplies since it's on a child. I'd like to prepare the tray before I leave for lunch,' Melody, the hematology technologist, said.

'Just the usual pediatric needles. Who's the patient?' she asked absentmindedly as she tidied her desk.

'Caitlin Burns.'

'What?' Her hands freezing in mid-air, she glared at Melody.

'Caitlin Burns.'

Thrusting her shoulders back like a general, Heather bit out a terse, 'Excuse me,' as she brushed past a startled Melody.

No wonder he'd given her a warm welcome, she silently grumbled, stomping her way toward Aaron's office for the second time in as many hours. She should have known he'd take the opportunity to rescind her decisions while she was gone. How many others would she discover?

Finding his office empty, she retraced her steps. Turning the corner into the lab, she ran smack dab into him.

'There you are!' he exclaimed, steadying her with his large hands on her shoulders. 'I was looking for you.'

Ignoring their audience, she blurted, 'Why are you meddling in my cases?'

CHAPTER EIGHT

'MEDDLING?'

Heather noticed Aaron's narrowed eyes and flared nostrils but her anger overrode caution. 'That's what I said. How many other decisions did you countermand while I was gone?'

With his mouth set in a grim line, he grabbed her upper arm and pulled her into the closest private space—the tiny room housing the equipment for the frozen sections.

'Hold it right there,' he retorted, blocking the closed door with his tall frame. 'I didn't meddle in your cases and I certainly didn't countermand any orders.'

'Then why is Caitlin Burns scheduled for a bone marrow today?' Heather thrust her hands into her coat pockets, balled her fists, and wished he'd sit down. It was difficult to vent her anger on someone towering over her.

'I was on my way to tell you when you started hurling accusations,' he ground out, his eyes changing to the dark blue color of thunderclouds ready to send down torrential rain.

In her fury, she refused to heed the warning signs of his rising temper. 'You knew Caitlin Burns was my patient and you deliberately went around me. I'm surprised you didn't do the exam while I was gone.'

'Enough,' he roared. 'Don't say another word.'

She clamped her jaw shut with his voice reverberating

138

in her ears, his fierce gaze suddenly making her feel like a rabbit stalked by a fox. She retreated two whole steps until she backed into a wall, aware that she'd pushed him too far with her criticism.

Aaron advanced until they stood almost nose to chest. 'Jim Wheeler came to me, not the other way round.' With anger dripping off every word, he summarized his conversation with the pediatrician. He finished with, 'I scheduled the test because of a specialist's recommendation, not because I wanted to take over your case. And as a matter of fact we *did* talk about proceeding immediately, but Jim agreed to wait until today out of courtesy to you.'

'Oh.' Heather wished she could crawl into a hole and lick her wounds. Her 'fight or flight' adrenalin surge dissipating, she felt as if all her energy had been siphoned away. Addressing the vee-neckline of his scrub suit, she apologized.

Raking his fingers through his hair, he studied her for a moment. 'What's really bothering you? I can understand your reaction with Emily. But after you learned I didn't toss her out on her ear I can't believe you'd be so willing to think the worst where Caitlin Burns is concerned.'

She clutched at her necklace. 'I suppose if anyone's shoved hard enough they'll eventually shove back.'

He tugged on her chin, drawing her face upwards. 'Have you been shoved, Heather?'

The compassion in his eyes nearly undid her. Yes, she screamed inside. Outwardly, she fidgeted. How could she explain that she felt as if she'd lost her place in the scheme of things, as if she was adrift in the Atlantic Ocean with only a plank to hold on to—a plank that seemed to splinter into smaller and smaller pieces?

He released her chin and leaned against the wall. 'You know, after I made my decision to leave Maryland, it was easy to feel threatened by the loss of what I considered to be *my* territory. I was gradually phased out of every project and committee I'd ever worked on. And I can understand your desire to defend what you have.' He paused. 'But it doesn't have to be that way, Heather. You have a place here for as long as you want. You don't have to look anywhere else.'

She jerked her head up, surprised that he'd pegged her so well. Without waiting for a comment—she didn't know what to reply anyway—he continued, 'I promised myself I wouldn't say anything, but to be quite honest I'm not looking forward to the day you'll leave.' His eyes softened. 'And I'm not referring to the fact that I'll have lost a very competent pathologist.'

Stunned by his admission, her shock soon gave way to the warm glow building inside. 'I've thought the same thing,' she confessed, feeling heat rise to her cheeks. 'But I can't give up my dream. . .'

'I understand, but if you should change your mind. . .'

Heather nodded as his voice trailed away. She knew that anyone else who felt as he did would have resorted to all sorts of high-pressure tactics to keep her at Plainview, but Aaron was allowing her the freedom to make her own decision.

With that thought, she realized why he'd never verbalized his feelings. In spite of his attraction, he didn't want to influence her. He must have suspected she was pulled in enough directions that she didn't need his rope added to the pile. Her respect for him grew, making her tally another reason to remain.

Her mental list of advantages versus disadvantages should have been making it easier to feel good about her decision to leave, but it wasn't. Mulling over her dilemma, she only caught the tail end of his comment.

'I'm sorry. What did you say?' she asked, pulling herself away from her introspection.

'If it's indicated, do you want to do Caitlin Burns' bone marrow, or should I?'

'I will,' she decided.

Aaron opened the door and stepped aside for Heather to precede him. 'I see everyone disappeared,' he commented wryly.

'They probably didn't want to be called as witnesses in a murder trial. As angry as we were, I'm sure they expected the worst. Especially after you dragged me into that cubbyhole,' she teased. Deep down, she knew she'd have turned beet-red if anyone had been present to watch their exit from the cubicle so she was glad that the staff had vacated the premises.

'Shall we show them that we're both still in one piece?' His mouth twisted and his eyes sparkled.

'We'd better if we don't want the security guards to come running.'

'There you are,' Jim Wheeler's voice echoed in the doorway. 'I've been looking for you.'

'We're on our way to see if they have Caitlin's CBC finished,' Aaron replied smoothly.

Heather wondered what Jim would say if he knew where they'd been during his search. Pointedly keeping her gaze directed away from Aaron, she allowed herself a small private smile and followed the two men down the hall to the hematology lab.

A few minutes later, they had their answers.

'I'll tell the Burnses the news and get them settled in one of the exam rooms,' Jim said. 'I'll wait for you there.'

'I'd hoped we could avoid this,' Heather said softly after Jim had left.

'We have no choice,' he reminded her.

'I know.'

During the brief walk to the emergency center, she braced herself for what lay ahead. Children weren't extremely cooperative, especially during a painful procedure. A light sedative helped, but it couldn't be very strong or it would affect the marrow, and that defeated their purpose. She wished there were a better way, one less traumatic, but there wasn't.

Outside the exam room, Aaron grabbed her elbow. 'Are you certain you want to do this?' His eyes reflected his concern. 'I'd be happy to——'

She shook her head. 'Thanks, but no, thanks.' She refused to succumb to her softer side. Caitlin was her patient, and she would see this through to the bitter end.

His hand fell away. 'Good luck,' he murmured before pushing the door open.

The tiny room was filled with the three physicians, two nurses, and Melody. 'Hi, Caitlin,' Heather said as she quickly arranged the child's bedclothes to suit her. 'Has Dr Jim told you what I'm going to do?'

Caitlin nodded, her large brown eyes wide and her bottom lip quivering. Heather glanced at the nurses and they sprang into action. One gently disengaged Mrs

Burns' hand from her daughter's and led the parents out of the room while the other stood in the spot they'd vacated.

Heather and Aaron donned their gowns, masks and gloves while Jim and the nurse visited quietly with Caitlin.

As Heather skirted the bed, she was glad that she'd talked with Caitlin before now. At least she wasn't a total stranger to the little girl.

Deafening her ears to the sobs bursting out of Caitlin's mouth, she requested the syringe filled with the local anesthetic and began her grisly task.

Soon it was over. The child's cries gradually died down, her body shaking less and less. Heather felt drained, and just as glad as the Burnses that this step was over.

'She did very well,' she remarked to the worried parents when they were allowed back into the room.

Letting Jim take over with the explanations, the two pathologists and Melody left ER. 'We'll be along later,' Aaron mentioned, steering Heather toward the doctor's lounge.

'OK. I'll get right on this,' the technologist promised before turning down another corridor.

'This isn't necessary,' Heather protested as Aaron opened the door and guided her toward an overstuffed chair.

'You need some time to unwind,' he stated, pouring coffee into a mug and handing it to her. 'This looks terribly strong, but it's the best I can do without sending Paul Carter into cardiac arrest.'

She smiled, imagining Carter's florid face if he discovered a bottle of whiskey on hospital property.

'This has been quite a day,' he sighed, sinking into an identical chair across from her.

'You can say that again,' she replied, sipping the dark brew. After hearing Caitlin's ear-splitting screams for twenty minutes, she found the quiet atmosphere soothing. As her defenses fell, so did her restraint. She'd wanted to delve into Aaron's past for some time, but had never had the nerve to address the subject. Now she did.

'Why haven't you remarried?' she asked, waiting for his response.

It came quickly. 'I never met a woman I wanted to tie my life—and Josh's—to forever. Having Mrs B around kept me from rushing into a relationship because I needed help with childcare and the housework.' He grinned. 'Of course that may all change now that I'm on my own.'

'Josh isn't a baby anymore,' she reminded him, caught up in her questioning and paying little attention to the mirth on his face.

'True, but I haven't developed a love for cleaning and I appreciate a tidy place as much as the next person.'

'So you *are* looking for a wife.' She shouldn't have been surprised. He was an attractive man and held a responsible position in a small community where family values were important.

'Actively hunting, no. But a man would have to be dead not to keep his eyes open for the right opportunity. And Heather——' he leaned forward, his elbows on his thighs with his hands clasped in front of his knees '—I'm not dead.'

His quiet assurance made her squirm. She could attest that he was a living, breathing male.

He straightened. 'I'm *not* looking for someone to cook and clean and do my laundry. I want her to share my life, not take care of my every need.' His eyes took on a gleam. 'Now that I think about it, that doesn't sound so bad after all.'

The teasing note in his voice lightened her mood. She grabbed the small pillow tucked behind her and threw it at him.

He caught it before it landed on his head. 'Keep this up and I won't ask you to see *The Taming of the Shrew* on Friday night.'

'How did you get tickets?' she squealed. 'I heard they'd sold out as soon as the box office announced that a Shakespearean troupe was scheduled.'

He rubbed his knuckles on his shoulders, as if polishing brass. 'I have my ways. So, would you like to go?'

'I'd love to,' she declared. Glancing at her watch, she asked, 'Do you suppose Melody and Kim have some slides ready for us by now?'

Aaron rose. 'As efficient as they are, I'd say so.'

Indeed, as he had predicted, Melody's films were stained, coverslipped and waiting beside Heather's microscope.

Heather took her time perusing the specimens, carefully counting and classifying the cell types present. When she finally finished, she jumped to her feet to find Aaron.

'I can't find Dr Spence, Ruth,' she said after she'd checked his usual haunts. 'Is he in a meeting?'

The secretary pointed down the hall. 'I thought I saw him in the chemistry section a few minutes ago.'

'Thanks.'

She found him in the area Ruth had mentioned. Walking closer, she overheard the words 'hepatitis C'.

'Do you have something interesting?' she asked, curiosity overtaking her.

Aaron nodded. 'Yes. You remember we had a patient scheduled last week for a liver biopsy? It showed signs of cirrhosis and, just as I'd suspected, Larry got a positive hepatitis C test result.'

'No kidding? We don't see that too often around here.'

'Keep me posted on Trowbridge's liver-function studies,' Aaron told the tech before ushering Heather out of the lab.

'I've just confirmed Caitlin Burns' diagnosis,' she mentioned proudly. 'No signs of leukemia.'

'That's wonderful.'

'Yeah, isn't it? Her cell counts fell within the acceptable ranges, and the stains show plenty of iron reserves. I suspect she's still suffering from some lingering after-effects of a virus. Maybe the viral cultures we ordered will give us some clues.'

'I'm glad you were right, for the Burnses' sake.'

Heather heard the distance in Aaron's voice and saw how he evaded her eyes. Instinctively she knew the reason.

She touched his forearm. 'I'm not angry that I did the procedure, Aaron, even if I did oppose it. I'm only sorry Caitlin had to suffer, even for a short time, but it couldn't be helped.'

His head turned and she fixed her calm gaze on his troubled one. 'I'm glad the Burnses won't feel like there's a time bomb ticking away in their daughter. I won't say I told you so, Aaron. You were right; I should have done this a week ago even without a specialist's recommendation. The entire time I studied this case I could only think of how devastated I'd feel if my wait-and-see attitude had delayed Caitlin's treatment.'

She watched the tension leave his face as he absorbed her reassurances. Lacing her arm around his, she tilted her head up to wink at him.

'It's past five o'clock. Shall we call it a day, Dr Spence?'

He smiled broadly. 'By all means, Dr Manning.'

'Thank goodness that was the last session,' Heather moaned as she kicked off her tennis shoes and collapsed on the sofa two weeks later.

'Yes, but when Aaron sees you in that shimmery red dress tomorrow night and drools over you like a kid outside a toy store right before Christmas you'll thank me,' Janet promised, curling up on the recliner.

Heather smiled. Some of the glances she'd inter-cepted lately, whether wearing baggy surgical garb or street clothes, had sent shivers down her spine. The strapless cocktail-length gown she'd splurged on was certain to make a memorable impression.

'What time will Aaron be by for you?'

'Six o'clock.'

'If you're not there by the time dinner is served at seven, I'll know you were detained. Zippers can be very tricky.' Janet winked.

'The dress has buttons, remember?' Heather said, her face warming at the implication.

'That's even better,' Janet declared.

'Would you stop?' Heather chided. Unfortunately the idea had taken root and images of them together filled her mind with lightning speed. She shivered, remembering how his special scent heralded his presence before his strong arms surrounded her on private occasions.

'You have been getting along rather well,' Janet pointed out.

'Yes, we have,' Heather admitted. Ever since their disagreement a few weeks ago, they'd spent a lot of their free time together. Although they nearly always included Josh in their plans, the evening set aside for the acting troupe's performance had been their first official date.

'I'm glad you're happy, Heather.'

She grinned. 'Me too.' There'd never been a period in her life this exhilarating; even the hectic days following her acceptance to med school seemed to pale in comparison. It was difficult to explain that she'd never felt more alive, and so she didn't try. The only bad moments she'd had were when worries about her future had surfaced, but she'd quickly pushed them aside in order to concentrate on the day at hand.

'Heard anything from your dad lately?'

'Not a word. But I'm sure I will soon.' Privately, Heather dreaded that moment. He'd want to know why she hadn't continued her job search, would consider her foolhardy for waiting on news from the two contacts she'd made.

Idly, she thumbed through the mail she'd dropped on the coffee table before dashing to her aerobics class. The first few pieces were the usual first-of-the-month bills and she laid them on a pile beside her purse.

'Anything interesting?' Janet asked.

'A jewelry circular.' Heather tossed the colorful advertisement to her friend. She quickly shuffled through the remainder of the stack, stopping short when the return address on the last one caught her eye.

Oklahoma City.

Papers fluttered to the floor as she clutched the pristine white envelope in her hand. Her future rested on the contents of this letter.

'What's wrong?'

Heather waved the note.

Janet untangled her legs and scooted to the edge of her seat. 'Is that what I think it is?'

'I'd say so.' Heather stared at it.

'Aren't you going to open it?'

Heather looked at her faithful confidante, feeling a satisfied smile creep across her face. While her heart fluttered in anticipation, she slid one finger under the flap and loosened the edge. With shaking fingers she withdrew the single page of heavyweight stationery and began reading.

The words blurred together as she read them a second time.

'Well?' Janet demanded after a minute had passed.

Heather folded the letter neatly and shoved it into its envelope. 'I didn't get the job,' she announced quietly.

'Oh, Heather. I'm so sorry.'

'I really thought I had a very good chance,' she mourned.

'They probably had a hard time making a decision. Weren't you expecting to hear something last week?' Without waiting for Heather's reply, Janet continued, 'What did the letter say?'

Heather plucked at a torn edge. 'The standard line about selecting another candidate and thanking me for my interest. I wouldn't be surprised if they'd promoted one of the assistants I'd met during my interview.'

'I really am sorry, honey.'

'Don't be. Rejection comes with the territory and I knew that before I began job-hunting.'

'Hey, you don't have to keep a stiff upper lip around me.'

'I know.' She sighed. 'Part of me wants to cry and another part is glad. After all, there were several aspects that I didn't like.'

'Then be thankful they didn't choose you. The people at Newton still have you under consideration, don't they?'

Heather nodded.

Janet threw up her hands. 'Then don't worry. There's hope. And in the meantime you can see if your relationship with Aaron will go anywhere.'

Heather thought a moment. 'Why is it that I can't seem to have both of my dreams? I mean, other women climb a career ladder and still have a family. You, for instance.'

Janet waved her hands in front of her. 'I'm only a lowly general practitioner, not chief of the service. Yes, I have a family but I've had to give up some things. Few people can have it all. The trick is in knowing what you want the most.'

Heather nodded. Unfortunately, she didn't know if she could sacrifice her career for Aaron, or vice versa. But one thing she did know, and that was that she could only count on herself.

The clock chimed seven times. 'Oh, my goodness.

Didn't you say you were taking the boys to the movie at seven-fifteen?'

'It's OK. Dave can handle them if you want me to keep you company,' Janet offered.

Heather rose and ushered her friend to the door. 'I'm fine. Really. Go on and have a good time.'

'Are you sure?'

'Absolutely.'

'Will you call Aaron? I'm sure he'll be glad to hear you won't be leaving in the near future,'

'Don't worry. I'll tell him.'

But after Janet left she stole outside to watch the fish and to think. After an hour of reliving her interview, she realized she wasn't as upset by the turn of events as she could have been. Perhaps subconsciously she'd known the Oklahoma job wasn't for her. The one in Newton did seem to fit her interests and personal working style much better.

Her face softened. She liked the idea of spending the next few weeks cultivating a relationship with Aaron. And if the job in Newton fell through she could always begin her search again.

With her heart lighter, she decided to wait and tell him the news tomorrow when she could do it face to face. She wanted to see if his reaction matched the one she envisaged.

'I heard from the practice in Oklahoma City,' she began nonchalantly the next day after lunch at her house. Out of the corner of her eye, she studied his response while refilling his glass with iced tea.

'Oh?' His face impassive, he reached for the sugar bowl.

She could tell he wasn't as unaffected as he appeared since he scooped three heaped teaspoons into the tumbler rather than his usual two level ones. She also could have sworn she saw a flash of panic in his blue eyes, and took pity on him.

'I wasn't chosen.'

His head jerked up. 'What?'

'I wasn't chosen,' she repeated, sitting down next to him at the kitchen table.

'How do you feel about it?' he asked, his tone wary.

Heather noticed that he didn't give the usual 'I'm sorry' platitude. Probably because he wasn't. 'I'm OK. I was disappointed at first, but after I thought about it I realized it's probably for the best.'

Aaron took her hand and covered it with both of his. 'I'm glad you're staying.'

'For now,' she said. 'I haven't given up my career plans. They're just on hold.'

The bleakness in his eyes had disappeared, replaced by something resembling excitement in spite of her proviso. 'I understand.' The brightness dimmed. 'Have you told your father yet?'

She shook her head as she chewed on her lower lip. 'I don't think he'll accept the news as well as I have. I'll wait until next week—I'm not in the mood for a confrontation today.'

'And what mood *are* you in?' he teased.

'Grass-planting,' she replied promptly. 'The fellow at the greenhouse said that fall was the best time and you did promise to help.'

'I know.' He faked a groan. 'I just hate to work too hard since I have such a big evening planned. I don't want to fall asleep in the middle of my prime rib.'

'You won't,' she promised, letting his joking protests fall on deaf ears as she pushed him toward the back door. 'It's only a small spot and it won't take us more than thirty minutes.'

The doorbell pealed and she halted. 'I'll be right out. The rake, grass seed and fertilizer are on the patio.'

But when she opened the front door and saw her visitor, all thoughts of yard work fled. She gulped, then cleared her throat. Her voice still came out sounding hoarse.

'Dad. What brings you here?'

The confrontation was about to begin.

CHAPTER NINE

'I THOUGHT it was time I paid a visit,' Richard Manning
declared, his male attendant cautiously wheeling his
chair through the doorway.

Heather's self-assurance ran out of her like water
down a drainpipe. 'You didn't drive here, did you?'

'Of course not. We flew into your airport, such as it
is, and rented a van. How the Federal Aviation Agency
can classify that oversized parking lot as an airstrip I'll
never know.'

'You're looking well, Dad.' She changed the subject,
well aware of her father's opinion of the small town
where she'd lived the past few years. His hair boasted a
great deal more gray, but she couldn't see that his
physical condition had changed since she'd last seen
him six months ago.

'Hmmph!'

She offered her hand to her parent's companion. 'I
don't believe we've met.'

'Parker Nelson,' he replied, his grip strong. 'I've only
worked for Dr Manning a few weeks.'

She wasn't surprised. Her father went through his
personal aides so fast, she couldn't keep them straight.
The outlandishly attractive salary was the only reason
he could find ready replacements.

'It's nice to meet you.'

'You're free to go, Nelson,' Manning instructed. 'But
be back in two hours. I don't want to miss our flight

home. There probably isn't a decent hotel within a hundred miles.'

Letting that remark pass, Heather glanced at the clock and marked the time. Did she have enough antacids stockpiled to endure his visit?'

'You're welcome to stay here, Parker.'

He declined, smiling. 'I'd like to drive around town. I've never been in this part of the country before.'

Sensing that he didn't hold the same jaundiced view of her town as his employer, she directed him to several local landmarks she thought he might enjoy. As Parker closed the door, she thought she saw relief spread across his face. She understood completely.

'I was on my way outside to help Aaron. We're planting grass,' she mentioned to her father.

'Aaron?' His bushy silver brows rose.

'Aaron Spence. The other pathologist.'

'Oh, yes.'

Her heart sank at the sound of distaste in his voice. He'd already judged Aaron and found him wanting. Rubbing her throat since she hadn't worn any jewelry, she wished Aaron were with her. Maybe his strength would help her deal with her father with the same self-assurance she had for her work.

'Fine helper you turned out to be,' Aaron accused without rancor from the doorway. 'I'm all——' When he saw that Heather wasn't alone, he stopped short. 'Oh, excuse me. I didn't know you had company.' After a closer look, he recognized the man in the wheelchair and his sympathy for Heather grew.

She seemed lost, her eyes reflecting a variety of negative emotions. Manning's unplanned visit had obviously thrown her off balance and Aaron decided to buy her some time to regain her poise. He came forward, extending his hand. 'You must be Dr Manning. Heather's told me a lot about you.' In deference to the man's arthritis, he kept his grip light. It was unfortunate that he had to meet the man after he'd been puttering with yard work.

'I've heard about you too,' Manning replied.

Aaron sat down across the room. The older man appeared much more imposing than in his photo. Smiling was probably as foreign to him as ballet dancing. After careful study, Aaron detected only a faint resemblance between father and daughter and decided that Heather must take after her mother.

'Dad flew in for a visit.'

A mental image of the grim-faced man cackling with glee on a motorized broom came to mind. Aaron wiped his mouth with his palm to stifle the smile. 'That's wonderful,' he said instead. 'Tonight is Plainview's hospital benefit. Will you be joining us?'

'No. I wasn't aware it was scheduled for this evening.' Manning's pointed glare at his daughter signified his disapproval. 'Regardless, I didn't come here to socialize.' He addressed Heather. 'I want to find out what you're doing.'

Her hand darted to the base of her throat and Aaron knew her skin would be raw by the time Manning left since she didn't have her favorite locket to toy with. He tried to defuse the situation. 'She made those stained-glass windows. Aren't they absolutely breathtaking?'

Richard Manning barely glanced at them before turning his beady eyes on his offspring. 'I'd like to speak privately.'

Heather visibly stiffened her shoulders. 'You can say anything you like in front of Aaron.'

'Maybe I should leave,' Aaron began, rising out of the chair. Manning's lack of response to her creative efforts irritated him and he didn't mind the idea of leaving before he said something he shouldn't. He didn't want to escalate the tension already hanging in the room like a zero-visibility fog.

'Please don't,' she said, her eyes begging.

He sat back down, realizing he couldn't leave her alone when she needed him.

'What have you heard from Oklahoma?' Manning demanded.

Heather's voice came out quiet, yet confident. 'They selected someone else. I just received my notice yesterday.'

Manning pursed his lips. 'And your other leads?'

'I haven't heard from the other hospital yet.'

'You only answered *two* ads?' he thundered. 'How do you expect to find something if you don't send your c.v. anywhere? At this rate you'll be ready to retire and still stuck in this—this first-aid station,' he stuttered.

Aaron clenched his jaw to keep silent, but he felt his blood pressure rise at the slur.

'Plainview is a very progressive hospital for this area,' Heather defended.

'No doubt,' Manning scoffed. 'Regardless, I have several people you can contact who are most interested in talking with you.' With his crippled fingers slowing his progress, he withdrew a list from his breast pocket.

'I don't want your help, Dad. I can do this myself.'

'Don't be stubborn, Heather. Take it.'

She refused.

Manning swore.

Aaron folded his arms across his chest to hide his tightened fists.

'Do you or do you not want to rise to the top?' Manning demanded.

'I want to do it my way,' she repeated.

Tension sizzled in the silence. 'You've changed, Heather. I used to be able to reason with you,' Manning said.

Manipulate her, you mean, Aaron thought.

'I suppose *he's* responsible,' Manning continued, jerking his head in Aaron's direction.

'No, he's not. I only want to make certain I'm doing the right thing.'

'You mean you don't know? After all the years of making plans, you don't know?' Manning's voice rose.

Aaron couldn't contain himself. Even though this wasn't his fight, he'd had enough. And from all indications Heather had too. 'It isn't unreasonable to reassess plans.' He spoke using the deadly tone he'd perfected.

'All the more reason why she needs guidance. Her brain's gone soft.'

'I don't think so,' Aaron corrected him. 'She's finally questioning herself about the goals she's been working toward. They aren't hers, they're yours.'

'I beg your pardon?' Manning sputtered. 'Everybody wants to climb to the top. Heather isn't any different.'

'Isn't she?' Aaron asked. 'The only problem is, there's always something higher, more prestigious to strive for and then when does it end? What will you push her into after she becomes chief? Chairman of the state medical society? Or US Surgeon General?'

Aaron heard Heather's gasp, but kept his attention on her father.

'I don't have to listen to this,' Manning retorted. 'Heather, tell him that his ridiculous ideas aren't true.'

Aaron glanced at her. Her eyes were wide, as if she'd seen something for the first time.

'Aren't they, Dad?'

Manning's jaw closed with a snap, and silence reigned for only a few seconds. 'I can see I've wasted my time coming here. You've chosen him over me. Just remember that when you're doing all the work and he's basking in all the glory.'

'But it isn't that way,' she protested. 'Aaron is——'

'Taking advantage of you,' Manning finished. 'And as long as he is you can consider yourself on your own. I'm washing my hands of you. Don't call me until you come to your senses.'

'What? You can't mean that,' she cried, jumping to her feet.

'I most certainly do.'

The doorbell rang and Manning wheeled himself to the door. Opening it, he barked at the man on the porch. 'Nelson, get me out of this place. Now.'

Parker swung into action, sending an apologetic look in Heather and Aaron's direction.

Once they were alone, Aaron pulled her into his embrace. 'He doesn't mean it. He'll regret his impulsiveness.'

Her smile was wan. 'No, he won't. My father could give lessons on holding grudges. I'm just sorry you had to hear that.'

'I'm glad you didn't have to face him alone. I thought you handled yourself very well.'

'Thanks,' she whispered. Tearing herself out of his grasp, she excused herself.

Taking advantage of her absence, he sprinted outside. Fueled by righteous anger, he strode to the driver's side of the van where Parker had thoughtfully rolled down his window. Aaron spoke loudly, knowing Dr Manning could hear him even if his efforts weren't acknowledged.

'Heather loves you. And because I love her I won't indulge my fondest wish to bloody your nose. But someday, when you're alone, compare what you have with what might have been.' He stepped back.

The elder man looked directly ahead, his face grim as he ordered, 'Drive, Nelson.'

Aaron walked inside just as Heather reentered the living room. 'Is he gone?' she asked, her eyes dull.

'Yes.' As he saw her distress, his chest ached.

'I can't believe he said those things,' she choked out.

He couldn't stand the way she stood, looking like the puppy nobody wanted. 'When people are hurt, they lash out.'

'But to totally reject his own child. . .' she began, pain evident in her voice.

He stepped closer, within easy reach. 'You aren't alone. You have Janet and Kim and countless other friends. And I'm here whenever you need me.'

With that, she walked into his waiting arms.

Heather colored under Aaron's appreciative male gaze when he arrived a few hours later for their evening engagement. He stared at her as if she were the Hope diamond, his eyes glistening with delight as he inspected her with all the care and delight of a jeweler. Her red dress swirled softly around her legs, the metallic threads woven through the fabric sparkling as she moved in the light.

'Simply breathtaking,' he finally pronounced.

'Thank you.' She smiled, feeling her spirits raise. 'You look rather dashing yourself.'

He wore a classic black tuxedo, but it molded his trim frame to perfection. Her first impression had been correct; he was positively stunning in formal wear. And the fact that he was *her* escort sent another shiver of excitement skipping through her.

'Are you certain you're up to this?' he asked as they left her house, a small frown marring his mouth.

'I'm fine,' she assured him. After her father had left, she'd soaked Aaron's shirt with her tears. He'd comforted her the rest of the afternoon, keeping her firmly tucked in his embrace while they talked about inconsequential things. He'd only left after she'd insisted that she needed time to get ready for the evening. 'I want to enjoy myself,' she added. For the next few hours she wanted to create some fabulous memories to replace the unpleasant ones made earlier in the day.

Before long, his car entrusted to a parking attendant, they joined the near-capacity crowd in the hotel's huge meeting room. She delighted in the feel of his hand resting lightly on her waist, his coat brushing against her bare shoulders. The light contact, combined with his aftershave wafting around her, sent electricity shooting across her nerve endings and she shivered in spite of the warm fall evening.

'Wow. This is quite a party,' Aaron remarked in her ear. 'It must have taken the decoration committee hours to get ready.'

Heather agreed. Silver and blue ballons covered the ceiling. Blue candles flickered on every table, reflecting light off the tiny foil stars scattered around the china place settings. A beautiful miniature castle stood at one end of the dais, with the theme of 'Dreams are for Everyone' glittering on the wall behind it.

She smiled and nodded at several couples as they meandered around. 'I'd say they outdid themselves. But then I shouldn't be surprised; this benefit is one of *the* social events of the year. Anyone can attend for the price of a ticket, but those with any social standing at all wouldn't miss it. See the two men over there? They're bankers.'

'And the group by the punch fountain?'

'Real estate. Have you met Harlan Gray, the hospital attorney?'

Aaron shook his head.

'He's the one with the red bow tie standing by the swan ice sculpture. The couple with him are also attorneys.'

'Who's the guy talking to Carter?'

Heather looked in the direction Aaron indicated. 'The old man?' she asked.

He nodded.

'That's Cyrus Fairbanks. He's been very generous in the past and I'm sure Carter is doing his best to coax another substantial donation. That lovely young redhead is Cyrus's wife.'

'No kidding? Talk about robbing the cradle,' he commented.

'I understand he threw quite a bash last April for their birthdays. He turned seventy and she hit twenty-one. Rumor says she's a model. I don't doubt it. She's a very beautiful woman.' Heather studied Mrs Fairbanks with a touch of envy. She would have loved to have her height and regal bearing.

'She is lovely,' Aaron agreed. 'But there's someone else who's much more attractive.'

'Where?' Without thinking, Heather craned her neck to catch a glimpse of the mystery female.

'She's right beside me,' he murmured.

She was already warmed by his words, and his whisper-soft breath in her ear was like setting a match to kindling. Gazing into his eyes, she felt her insides turn into molten fire at the look she saw there.

'Aaron,' Paul Carter's voice came, interrupting her thoughts. 'I'm glad I found you. There are some people you simply have to meet. Won't you excuse us, Heather?' Without waiting for a reply, he grabbed Aaron's arm and pulled him along.

Aaron glanced over his shoulder and she mouthed, 'Have fun.' She'd known it would only be a matter of time until Carter commandeered Aaron into making his rounds. While Aaron disappeared into the throng, she sauntered through the crowd, visiting briefly with a number of acquaintances she encountered.

'Would you care for some wine?' a waiter asked, offering a tray.

She selected a glass, more to keep her hands busy than out of a desire for a drink. It would also keep her from being targeted by every server that passed by.

With great relief, she saw Janet and headed towards her.

'Lose Aaron already?' Janet asked.

'Sort of,' Heather answered drily. 'Carter's busy showing him off to his cronies. Where's Dave?'

'He's checking in with the boys. Say, was I right? Did Aaron drool when he saw you in that dress?'

Heather smiled, recalling the instant she'd opened the door. The memory of his slow perusal made her temperature rise. 'Let's just say our aerobics class was a good investment.'

'I knew it,' Janet crowed. 'Next time you'll be begging *me* to go with you.'

'Not a chance.' Heather sipped her wine while scanning the crowd. Just when she was about to give up, she caught a glimpse of Aaron in the distance. Immediately her heart danced as she watched him singlemindedly skirt tables and chatting guests to reach her side. The joy on his face matched her own and she suddenly knew that she loved him.

She couldn't believe it had happened, considering all the conflicts between them. And she'd certainly never dreamed that the attraction she had for him would blossom into love.

Now what would she do?'

'I thought I'd never find you,' Aaron declared, moving in so close, she could feel his warmth.

Her worries flitted away. 'I was thinking the same thing. Did you meet all of Paul's important people?'

'I hope so,' he replied fervently. 'I only got away because I told him I needed to find my table.'

'Ladies and gentlemen, welcome to Plainview's eighth annual hospital benefit,' Paul Carter announced over the loudspeaker. 'If you'll find your seats, I believe they're ready to serve dinner.'

The Franklins and Jim Wheeler, along with his guest, Julie, sat with them. Heather joined in the dinner conversation flowing around the table, but her senses simmered underneath her lightheartedness. Aaron's knee rested against hers and made her impatient for the dancing to begin. At least then she'd have a legitimate excuse to be in his arms.

At the close of the meal, Judith Dalton came to the microphone and thanked everyone for their generous contributions. 'We'd like to introduce a few new faces to Plainview Medical Center since our last benefit—Dr Jerry McCain, our new obstetrician, and Dr Aaron Spence, our head of pathology.'

Aaron rose to his feet, along with his colleague, and graciously accepted the applause. While Heather clapped, she realized she was glad he'd come to Plainview, even though his presence had put her own aspirations on hold. Deep in thought, she hardly noticed that Judith had finished her speech until the crowd started to disperse and Jim and his date rose from the table. 'No art lovers here?' the pediatrician joked.

'We'll pass,' Janet replied.

'What about you, Heather? The auction or dancing?' Aaron asked.

'Dancing,' she leaned closer to say, already shivering with anticipation.

'Good. I was hoping you'd choose that.' He draped his arm around her shoulders and they remained behind.

While they visited with the Franklins, Aaron's fingers traced a slow path on her upper arm. Her skin tingled, and she could hardly focus on the conversation. The longer they sat, the more she wanted to feel his hard body against hers, his arms around her.

When the music started and the lights dimmed, he

led her on to the dance floor without asking. His eyes smoldered with fire, providing evidence that his desire matched her own.

'My favorite,' he murmured in her ear during a slow waltz.

'Mine too,' she replied, thrilled to be held against his solid chest while he guided her across the floor. 'It's been ages since I've danced.'

'You're doing very well.'

'I have a good partner.'

When the song changed to a lively fox-trot, he stopped and looked apologetic. 'Sorry. I never learned those steps.'

She smiled. 'I can use a drink anyway.' Although she'd been taught the fox-trot, the polka and the Charleston in her younger days, she preferred waltzes. And as the evening wore on the musicians catered to her silent wishes.

When the band leader announced their final number, Heather was surprised. Time had passed so quickly, she could hardly believe it was well past midnight.

The house lights brightened after the last strains faded away. Heather and Janet located their purses underneath a chair and the two couples headed for the nearest exit. 'Where's Josh tonight?' Heather asked.

'He's sleeping over at Kevin's,' Aaron replied, slinging his jacket over his shoulder.

Out of the corner of her eye she glimpsed the satisfied smirk on Janet's face. Her friend had obviously arranged circumstances so that the evening wouldn't have to end prematurely.

'Shall we stop at the Cattleman's Club for a drink?' Dave asked.

Janet responded quickly. 'I'd rather call it an evening. All that dancing wore me out.'

Dave looked puzzled. 'But you just told me——'

Her elbow cut off his breath. 'I'm tired, honey. And you are too.'

Dave finally understood. 'Oh, yeah. That's right. It has been a busy day. See you tomorrow, Aaron. Better not come by too early, though—I'm sure the boys will sleep late,' he said as he ushered Janet into the darkness.

'Either they wanted to be alone or they wanted us to be alone,' Aaron remarked while they waited for the attendant to deliver his car.

'I think you're right.' She didn't particularly want to go out for a drink, but she knew she didn't want the evening to end. If they went home—his or hers—she knew they wouldn't spend time discussing the latest advances in pathology. She shivered, anticipating his touch.

'Are you cold?' Without waiting for her reply he swung his coat over her. She pulled the collar tightly around her neck. With a sigh of pleasure, she buried her nose in the fabric.

'Did you enjoy yourself?' she asked after the car had arrived and he'd helped her inside.

'More than I ever dreamed. And you?'

'It was fabulous.'

'I didn't realize you loved to dance. We'll have to do this more often.'

When they were within view of her home, memories of her father burst into living color and her euphoric mood vanished with the speed of a falling star. Suddenly it became imperative that Aaron should linger and recast the evening's magic spell.

As he escorted her to the door, doubt reared its ugly head and she fretted over semantics. How did one ask a date to spend the night? She was being ridiculous, she knew, but after suffering her father's rejection hours earlier she couldn't help worrying that Aaron would reject her as well.

'Won't you come in?' she finally blurted. With her mouth dry and her heart thumping so hard she was certain he could hear it, she steeled herself for his reply.

CHAPTER TEN

'If I do, I'll want breakfast,' Aaron warned, his eyes dark in the moonlight.

Heather let out the breath she hadn't realized she'd been holding. How foolish to be so nervous and fearful. 'Will bacon suit you?'

His teeth gleamed white. 'Perfect.'

A few steps later they were inside the dimly lit room with the door closed. She tossed her purse on to the sofa and peeled off his jacket. Her arms suddenly prickled with a mixture of cold and anticipation.

He stepped forward and gently caressed her bare shoulders. 'Making love isn't something I take lightly, so are you sure this is what you want? You don't have to prove anything, you know.'

How had he known she'd needed to reaffirm her worth? She tilted her head up. 'I've wanted this all evening.'

His hand moved to her bodice. With his eyes locked on hers, he gave her one last opportunity to refuse.

She smiled and worked the buttons on his shirt. He reached behind her to undo the fastenings and soon the red dress whispered softly into a puddle around her feet. Stepping out of it, she grabbed his hand and led him into her bedroom.

Sweeping her on to the bed, he kissed her thoroughly. His hands roamed at leisure when bare skin finally met bare skin, driving her close to the edge of sanity.

She reciprocated, his throaty moans testifying to her success. At long last, they scaled the heights before drifting ever so slowly back to earth in each other's arms.

'What should we do today?' Aaron asked later that morning as he scrambled the eggs. Although Heather wore a fresh pair of jeans and a pullover, he wore his now rumpled tuxedo trousers and equally wrinkled silk shirt. The latter, however, hung open, and she enjoyed the sight.

'I don't care. We could hop on our bikes and zip around town,' she replied, removing the crisp bacon from the microwave tray.

'You want exercise?' He quirked an eyebrow.

'We can't leave Josh with Janet and Dave forever, you know,' she teased, thrilled that he wanted her again.

'I suppose not.' He sighed dramatically. 'But the idea does have merit.'

She stood on tiptoe and planted a kiss on his woebegone face. 'You're an intelligent man. I'm sure you'll figure something out so we can have some private time. You know the old saying—where there's a will, there's a way.'

'You're so right,' he said, grabbing her around the waist for a quick hug.

'So what's on the agenda for tomorrow?' he asked while they ate their breakfast.

'I don't recall seeing anything too terrible on the surgery schedule. I'll probably be late getting to the lab, though. Milton Evers is scheduled for prostate surgery.'

'Isn't he the one of the men with the positive PSA test?'

She swallowed the forkful of fluffy eggs, then nodded. 'His MRI indicated the presence of a tiny mass but his doctor didn't detect any abnormalities during his exam.'

'Isn't it amazing how technology has improved our diagnoses? Without the Magnetic Resonance Imaging, Evers wouldn't know he had a problem until it was possibly too late.'

'I know. Even though we can't afford to have our own MRI machine, I'm glad the mobile unit comes to Plainview twice a week.' She got up and refilled her coffee cup. 'Would you like more?'

'Just a little.' He held out his mug. 'Then I'll help you with the dishes before I pick up Josh.'

Heather switched on the radio while they worked, hoping to hear an updated weather report. But in the middle of the headline news segment a latebreaking bulletin made them both freeze.

'A Holloway Airlines jet carrying over two hundred people crash-landed early this morning in the Arizona desert. The cause is unknown and aviation officials are searching for the plane's black box. Teams of federal investigators will be arriving throughout the day to sift through the wreckage. It's unknown how many of the passengers survived. In other news. . .'

'Oh, no,' she mourned. 'All those poor people.'

Aaron dried his hands on a towel and buttoned his shirt. 'I've got to get home. They're probably trying to reach me.'

Remembering he was a member of a team called specifically for such disasters, she scurried into the bedroom to retrieve his jacket and tie. Understanding his need for haste, she stood at the door with his clothes.

'Aren't you coming?' he asked, sounding surprised.

'I didn't know. . . Yes, I'll come.'

He drove on the fringes of the speed limit and they walked inside just in time to hear the phone ringing. 'Spence here,' he barked.

Heather waited, studying his expression for a clue. But his face remained impassive while he listened to the caller. She knew without asking, or hearing, that he would be leaving. His next sentence confirmed it.

'I'll take the next flight out,' he stated before replacing the receiver. Turning to her, he said somewhat apologetically, 'I have to go.'

'I know. How long will you be gone?'

He shrugged. 'A week, give or take a few days.'

'I'll help you pack.'

Fifteen minutes later, he was ready. Heather had called the airport and booked him on a flight leaving within the hour. Before they left the house, he tucked her under one arm.

'This isn't how I'd planned to spend the next few days,' he said, caressing her face with his fingertips. 'I wanted a few more hours like the ones we had.'

She held his palm against her cheek, memorizing the feel of his hand. 'Me too.'

He snapped his fingers as if he'd just thought of something. 'I've got to make arrangements for Josh.' He shook his head. 'I've always had Mrs B around to take care of things so I never worried when I had to leave unexpectedly.'

Without hesitation, she offered, 'If it's OK with you, he can stay with me. Or if he'd prefer to be at home I'll stay here. I'm sure Janet and Dave will help, too.'

'I can't ask you to do that.'

'You didn't. I volunteered. Now, if you want to see Josh before I take you to the airport, we'd better go.'

Once again, Aaron defied the speed limit and they reached the Franklins' house in record time. After a hasty explanation, they left for Plainview's tiny airport and entered the terminal just as Aaron's small plane taxied to the one and only departure gate.

'Geez. I bet it doesn't even have a flight attendant,' Josh remarked when they walked on to the tarmac.

'It doesn't,' Aaron remarked drily. 'Now, you mind Heather while I'm gone,' he told his son, hugging him.

'Aw, Dad,' Josh moaned.

Aaron turned to Heather and grabbed both hands. 'I really hate to leave. Talk about rotten timing.'

'Disasters never have good timing.' She smiled, trying to keep the tears at bay. Goodbyes were always difficult, and she hated them.

'I'll call whenever I can.'

'We'll be waiting. And don't worry, Josh and I will take good care of each other. Hurry home.'

Aaron looked at his son, then back at her. His lips lingered against hers for a few seconds before he stepped away. Bounding up the portable stairs, he disappeared.

Heather and Josh went inside the terminal. By unspoken agreement, they waited until Aaron's plane took off. When it finally soared into the sky, she offered a silent prayer for his safe return.

Making her rounds early Wednesday morning, Heather had just passed the fourth-floor nurses' station when Janet fell into step beside her. 'Have you heard from Aaron lately?' she asked.

Heather shook her head. 'Not since he called Sunday evening to tell us he'd arrived. According to the papers, the death toll stands at two hundred and fifteen, so I imagine he's working night and day to identify the bodies.'

'I'm sure he'll call when he can,' Janet encouraged. 'Why don't you and Josh come over for supper tonight?'

'I'd love to, but I promised Josh we'd order pizza.'

'OK. Maybe another night.'

'It's a deal.'

'How are you two getting along?'

'Great,' Heather boasted. 'He's a good kid.' Her only real problem—if it could be called that—was sleeping in Aaron's bed without him while surrounded by his lingering scent.

'Well, if you need anything, you know where to find us.'

Janet went on her way while another step brought Heather to her destination. She pushed open the door and found her patient sitting in bed. 'Good morning, Mr Evers. You're looking perky this morning.'

'Why, hello, Doc.' Using his remote control, Milton muted the television. 'I feel better than I thought I would. And even after surgery I'm still in better condition than most of those poor people.' He motioned to the set and Heather instinctively glanced in that direction.

A reporter faced the viewers, with twisted pieces of airplane wreckage visible in the background. Firemen, policemen and other emergency service personnel scurried past the live camera. 'One of our doctors is there,' she mentioned, hoping to catch a glimpse of Aaron.

'No kidding? I can't imagine how those guys stomach the job. All those mangled bodies. . .' He shook his head.

The silent picture flashed to another story and Heather, a little disappointed that she hadn't seen Aaron, addressed Mr Evers. 'I hear you're going home today.'

'You bet. By the way, I understand you're the one responsible for having the PSA test available at the health fair.'

'In a manner of speaking.' She didn't want to take full credit since the final decision had rested with Aaron.

'Well, you saved my life,' he declared. 'Without that test, I wouldn't have gone to the doctor and he wouldn't have found the cancer at such an early stage.'

She brushed aside his thanks. 'It was a team effort.'

'Now don't be modest, Doc. I know there's a huge list of people who were involved and I'm glad they did a good job, but you're the one who started it all.'

Milton's vehemence made her grin. Sensing that she couldn't dissuade him, she gracefully answered, 'I'm glad your case turned out well. Take care of yourself.'

'I will, Doc,' he promised.

Riding high on Mr Evers' praise, Heather returned to the lab, wishing that Aaron were across the hall rather than hundreds of miles away. She wanted to share her patient's exuberance but doing it over the telephone hours from now would make the experience lose some of its flavor.

Throughout the day she caught herself remembering Saturday evening, recalling in vivid detail Aaron's appearance the moment she'd realized she loved him. Now, as then, the image she'd captured in her mind sent delight winging through her soul.

Late in the afternoon, while she was reviewing the latest liver-enzyme report in Theodore Trowbridge, the telephone shrilled. 'Hello?' she answered absent-mindedly.

'Dr Manning? This is Mark Wilson, from Newton. How are you today?'

Heather jerked to attention. Her heart raced and she struggled to sound calm. 'I'm fine, thank you.'

'I'm calling about our chief pathologist's position. I'd like to offer it to you.'

She could hardly hear the details over the excitement rushing through her ears. Her dream had come true, and *she* had done it, not her father. She couldn't wait to tell Aaron.

His familiar face appeared and her eagerness faded. Once again, the dilemma she'd ignored these past few weeks reared its head. But this time she had to make a decision.

'Your offer sounds very good, but I'd like to have some time to think about it,' she said. 'I'll give you my answer on——' she thought fast '—Monday.'

'I look forward to hearing from you,' Wilson said.

She cradled the receiver. What was she going to do?

Agonizing over the question, she still hadn't reached

a decision by the time she arrived at Aaron's home. There she found a note tacked on to the refrigerator. 'At Kevin's. Home by six. Don't forget pizza.' She smiled, admitting to herself that she liked motherhood even if it was only temporary.

Before she could place the order, the phone rang. 'Spence residence,' she answered crisply.

'Heather. It's good to hear you,' a familiar baritone replied.

'Aaron. How are you?' She felt so happy, she thought she'd float to the ceiling.

'Tired, but fine.'

'It's pretty awful, isn't it?' she asked.

'It would have to improve in order to be awful.'

'Are you getting any rest?'

'Some. Most of us are anxious to finish.'

'When will you come home?'

'It's too soon to say. Hopefully by the middle of next week. But enough about me. How's Josh?'

'Just fine. He's over at Kevin's and he'll be sorry he missed you.'

'What's going on in Plainview?'

'Let's see. Dave removed Milton Evers' prostate and he's doing well. Ted Trowbridge's liver enzymes are coming down nicely, and Martin Jenner is responding well to chemotherapy.' She hesitated. Should she tell him about her job offer? Unwilling to give him another worry, she also knew that if she accepted the position she didn't want to inform him afterwards. He deserved a forewarning, especially in the light of their intimate relationship.

'The administrator from Newton offered me the chief pathologist's position,' she blurted.

There was a long silence. 'He did? Did you accept?'

She heard the wariness in his voice. 'I told him I'd give my answer on Monday.'

'I see.' Silence had never seemed so loud. 'Would you be happy there?' he asked.

'I think so,' she replied slowly. 'They've offered a generous salary and several other perks that are difficult to refuse.'

'There's something I have to tell you,' he began.

She couldn't hear the rest of his statement over the commotion at his end of the line. 'What did you say?' she asked, straining her ears.

'I've got to go,' he shouted over the noise. 'Don't do anything until I get back.'

Before she could answer, their connection was broken. Puzzled by his request, Heather replaced the receiver.

In Arizona, Aaron muttered a few choice words as he limped back to the makeshift morgue. He'd planned to take a few extra hours to relax and pamper his aching knee, but Heather's announcement had filled him with too much nervous energy to do either. Instead, he dug in his pocket for a pain pill.

If he completed a few more cases now, he might move his departure time forward. He poured himself another mug of coffee, strong enough to stand on its own, and began to sort through X-rays and dental records on the ill-fated passengers. If he kept busy, he couldn't dwell on the fact that his life was crumbling before his eyes since at the moment he was powerless to stop it.

* * *

'I've finally made up my mind, Janet,' Heather announced. 'After mulling it over all weekend, I'm going to call Mark Wilson tomorrow and accept the position.' Perhaps by verbally committing herself to someone the niggling doubts in her mind would disappear.

'I see. And what about Aaron?'

'What about him?' Heather inwardly winced at her defensive note.

'How will he feel? I mean, I thought you two were serious about each other.'

'I know I love him, but he's never mentioned he wants a commitment. He's had plenty of opportunities.'

Janet shrugged. 'Words can be meaningless, but actions reflect a person's true feelings. Maybe he's afraid to let you know how deeply he feels, thinking that years from now you'll hate him for having to give up your dream.'

'Medicine's the only thing I know. Being a wife or a mother is totally foreign to me. If you'll recall, role models were in short supply at my house.'

'It's foreign to all of us, even with ideal family situations,' Janet replied drily. 'But if you love each other your instincts will overcome your fear. Believe me.'

Long after Josh was fast asleep that night, Heather lay in Aaron's bed wide awake. Questions tumbled through her mind as fast as blood in a cell counter. Did Aaron's insistence that they had to talk mean that he planned to state unequivocally that he wanted her to stay? And would love be enough not only to tear down the career wall she'd been hiding behind, but also to teach her how to be a good wife and mother? Was she willing to work for a dream of her own?

Peace stole into her heart and a smile came over her face as she made her decision. Hurry home, Aaron, was her silent plea before she closed her eyes, when she awoke, and again when she peered out of the histology-room window a few hours later.

'I don't like the look of those clouds swirling around,' Heather told Kim. 'I hope Josh took his jacket today.'

Kim stopped her task to see for herself. 'You're right, those are nasty-looking. And look at the trees swaying. I'm surprised they haven't lost their leaves.' Turning to Heather, she asked, 'Did you make your call yet?'

Heather nodded. 'I decided it was pointless to wait so I telephoned a few minutes ago. I hope I won't regret it.'

'You won't,' Kim predicted. 'Does Dr Spence know that you're——?'

A voice over the loudspeaker interrrupted. 'T-alert. T-alert. This is not a drill.'

The two women looked at each other. 'Tornado? In September?'

'The official season is from March to October,' Kim reminded her. 'I guess we'd better batten down the hatches, so to speak.'

Heather hurried to her office for her portable radio before joining the staff already congregating in the windowless hallway. Employees from the doctors' offices above added to their number since the area— because of its location on the lowest level of the building—served as the designated tornado shelter. She could hear the wind's roar and the civil-defense sirens screaming above the muffled voices.

The disc jockey gave a running commentary about the storm, occasionally speaking live to the weather-spotters scattered throughout the city.

Suddenly the noise became deafening, like a freight train rolling past full steam ahead. Someone began sobbing. Bracing herself for the worst, Heather prayed for Josh's safety, adding a heartfelt sentence for Aaron if he was on his way home.

'What do you mean we're not leaving yet?' Aaron demanded of the airline-ticket agent. 'We've already been delayed for over an hour.' He was tired, hungry, and desperately in need of a shave. After working twenty-hour stretches for the past seven days, he wanted to get home and get there now.

'I'm sorry, sir, but planes can't fly in a tornado,' the young woman answered.

'Tornado?'

'I'm afraid so. The Weather Bureau has reported several tornado sightings in the Plainview area, and apparently one has touched down.'

'Where? Were there any casualties?' he demanded.

'I don't have that information, sir.'

'How soon can we leave?'

'The tower will give clearance as soon as it's feasible,' the agent replied patiently.

Upset by the news, Aaron paced the floor like an expectant father. Driving was out of the question since it would take hours; he'd get home faster even if he waited. Dammit, he wanted some news, some idea of where the tornado had hit. Had it been in town, or a farmer's field? A crop could be replaced, but Josh and Heather could not. Oh, God, keep them safe, he prayed.

The collective sigh of relief everyone breathed when the operator announced the all-clear disappeared a minute later when Heather instructed them to implement the disaster plan. Staff members scurried to their assigned stations and Heather dashed to the emergency room, ready to lend her skills for triage.

'The middle school was hit,' Linc Hayes, the ER physician, announced to the doctors assembling for duty.

'Oh, God,' Heather breathed. Josh. And Kevin.

'There are about three hundred kids in the whole school,' he continued, 'but the police dispatcher said only the west-wing annex was seriously damaged. No one knows how many students were there at the time.'

The sound of ambulance sirens grew louder, then stopped. 'Let's go, people,' Linc shouted as the doors burst open and the first of the injured were wheeled in.

The next few hours were hectic as Heather and the other physicians diagnosed broken bones and concussions, removed splinters, stitched up cuts, and soothed the children as best they could. Stretchers and wheelchairs took up every available space and as quickly as one patient was treated another took his place. While she worked, she kept her eyes and ears open for news about Josh.

'Hey, Doc? Can you take this one? He's pretty bad,' a paramedic motioned to Heather. 'His pressure is dropping. I'm sure he has internal injuries—we found him under a ceiling beam.'

The boy's dark hair made her think of Josh. But he wasn't and her heart settled down to a near-normal pace. She quickly palpated the boy's abdomen, carefully noting the bruises. 'I think he's ruptured his spleen. Draw blood for a CBC, clotting times, and a type and crossmatch. Then get him up to Surgery. See if the police can locate his parents.'

Dave walked by, his scrubs stained with blood. Heather pulled him toward her young patient. 'You're the man I need. I have a possible splenectomy here.'

He quickly performed his own examination while the lab technician drew blood. 'I'd say you're right. Get him upstairs stat,' he told the orderly. 'I'm on my way.'

Janet burst through the doors. 'Has Kevin come in?' she asked breathlessly.

'I don't think so. Neither has Josh. I guess that's good news.'

Janet looked grim. 'I hope so.'

Another hour went by. Heather had just finished cleaning and suturing a long jagged cut on a teacher's arm when she saw Kevin. He was leaning on Josh as they hobbled through the doors with a policeman, each disheveled and bloodstained. 'Janet,' she shouted above the din, relieved that the boys were safe and concerned about their condition. Grabbing the only available wheelchair, she maneuvered her way through the human obstacle course with Janet on her heels.

'What happened? We were so worried about you,' the women asked simultaneously as they eased a white-faced Kevin into the chair. Heather grabbed Josh's arm to steady him.

'We were the last ones out of the room when all of a sudden the windows broke and desks started flying around,' Josh reported, equally pale under his smudges. 'One hit us both.'

'My chest hurts, Mom,' Kevin whimpered.

Immediately Janet whisked her son away to Radiology.

'How do you feel, Josh?' Heather asked, leading him to an open spot on the floor. Running her hands along his extremities, she searched for broken bones and other injuries.

'My shoulder and neck hurt.'

Certain he had a broken collarbone, she sent him to Radiology with another nurse, promising to be there as soon as she could. He'd no sooner disappeared through the double doors than she heard her name called. When she turned round and saw the person striding forward singlemindedly joy coursed down to her toes.

'Aaron,' she breathed, walking into his outstretched arms and accepting his hungry kiss.

'Thank God you're all right,' he said when they came up for air. Immediately he held her at arm's length and she saw that his face was lined with stubble and etched with worry. 'I heard about the middle school. Have you seen Josh?'

She smiled through her tears of happiness. 'I just sent him to X-Ray with a fractured clavicle, but other than that he's fine.'

His shoulders slumped with relief and his eyes closed as he undoubtedly offered a silent prayer of thanks. 'I'd have arrived sooner but the plane wouldn't leave Denver until the weather cleared.'

'I'm glad you're here now.' She pushed him toward Radiology. 'Your son is waiting for you.'

'Don't go away,' he ordered.

'I won't,' she promised before watching him limp away.

Sinking on to a chair, she lowered her head and attributed her lightheadedness to relief that the people she cared about had passed through this experience relatively unscathed. She drank a cup of orange juice that some thoughtful nurse pressed into her hand. By the time the next ambulance arrived, she felt rejuvenated.

Janet returned, looking relieved. 'Kevin has a few broken ribs, but luckily his lungs weren't punctured. I saw Aaron and he's settling the boys at my house. He wanted to stay but Linc told him things were under control right now and asked if he'd mind relieving us later. I suspect he thought Aaron wasn't ready to tackle another disaster without some rest first.'

'I'm glad,' Heather replied. 'I know his knee was hurting terribly when I saw him earlier.'

But it wasn't much later when Aaron returned, brushing aside Linc's—and Heather's—protests to do his fair share.

They worked for hours, stopping only when the stream of patients finally dwindled to a trickle.

'You did a good job,' Linc told them gruffly, his face weary. 'Your replacements have arrived, so beat it.'

'You're right. It's time to go home,' Aaron announced from behind. 'I heard we treated more than a hundred children, and most of them were dismissed.'

'That's pretty good,' Heather declared.

'We were lucky the kids were in the main building,' Aaron remarked, rubbing his knee. 'As it was, we still ended up with over two dozen in a critical condition, and one fatality—the custodian.'

Janet nodded. 'I'm going to check on Dave before I leave. See you later.'

'I'll drive you home,' Aaron told Heather.

'OK. How's your knee?'

'Fine.'

'What a day,' she sighed as she got into his car. 'I haven't worked like this since medical school.'

'No kidding. Thank goodness we don't have to cope with these situations very often.'

'You must be exhausted after working on that disaster and then coming home to one,' Heather mentioned, noticing that he took the route to his house.

'I'll live. I'm just glad to be back.'

Aaron parked in the garage and ushered her inside. Keeping his grip on her arm, he said, 'We need to talk.'

She blinked. 'It's two in the morning. Can't it wait?'

'No.'

Sinking on to a chair, she stared up at him expectantly.

'Did you make your phone call?' he asked, his mouth set in a grim line as he towered over her.

'Yes and no. I called, but the administrator wasn't in. I left a message with his assistant.'

His shoulders slumped. 'Too late,' he muttered to himself, raking his hands through his hair as he plopped down on the nearby sofa. 'Too damn late.'

Her heart softened at the sight of his dejection. 'I refused their offer.'

His head jerked up and his gaze met hers. 'What?'

Coming to his side, she grabbed his hands and held them tightly. 'I told them no.'

'But I thought you wanted the job?'

She smiled at his incredulous tone. 'I thought so too,

but I'm happy with the one I have. Thinking about my mother made me realize that life is so very short and exceedingly precious. The storm and the air crash emphasized that.' He nodded while she continued, 'I want to live out my own dreams. I can't settle for those of my father.' In the next instant she found herself with her nose buried in his chest.

'Thank God,' he sighed. 'I love you, Heather. I've wanted to tell you that for so long, but I couldn't. Your father pressured you enough without me adding more.'

'I love you too, Aaron,' she said, resting her cheek against his soft shirt. 'I had to refuse the offer; I couldn't imagine living anywhere without you. I suppose, subconsciously, that was the reason I didn't want to send applications all over the country.'

'Josh told me he liked having you here,' he mentioned. 'In fact, he suggested I quit fooling around and marry you.'

Surprise made her stiffen. 'Oh, he did?'

'So what do you say?' Are you interested in handling a few more duties, like those as my wife and Josh's mother?' He tipped her chin up so that his slate-blue eyes could search her face.

'I'd be delighted,' she said, 'provided Josh can have brothers and sisters.'

'Absolutely,' he declared, his face lighting up. 'We have to give your father an excuse to visit.'

Her smile died. 'I don't think he'll care,' she whispered, feeling a lump she couldn't swallow form in her throat.

'He will,' Aaron predicted. 'And he does.'

'You keep saying that, but——'

He pressed an index finger to her mouth, effectively

cutting off her objection. 'I came home to get Josh a change of clothes and your father called just as I walked in the door. He'd been trying to reach you ever since he heard about the tornado, but you obviously weren't at your place and he couldn't get through to the hospital.'

'He actually telephoned?' Hope stirred in her chest.

Aaron nodded, his eyes filled with compassion. 'After I explained you were fine he broke down. You two definitely need to have a heart-to-heart talk.'

'I'll call him right away,' Heather promised.

He pulled her close and nuzzled her neck. 'As you said earlier, it's two in the morning. He's probably asleep.'

'You're right,' she answered breathlessly, feeling his lips work magic. 'I'd rather not talk now anyway.'

'You've read my mind.'

His mouth covered hers and she knew, without any doubt, that she'd made the right decision.

One of her very own dreams was coming true. The rest were sure to follow.

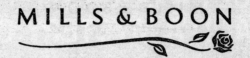

MILLS & BOON

LOVE CALL

The books for enjoyment this month are:

NEVER SAY NEVER	Margaret Barker
DANGEROUS PHYSICIAN	Marion Lennox
THE CALL OF DUTY	Jessica Matthews
FLIGHT INTO LOVE	Meredith Webber

Treats in store!

Watch next month for the following absorbing stories:

A FAMILIAR STRANGER	Caroline Anderson
ENCHANTING SURGEON	Marion Lennox
DOWNLAND CLINIC	Margaret O'Neill
A MATTER OF ETHICS	Patricia Robertson

GET 4 BOOKS AND A MYSTERY GIFT

Return this coupon and we'll send you 4 Love on Call novels and a mystery gift absolutely FREE! We'll even pay the postage and packing for you.

We're making you this offer to introduce you to the benefits of Reader Service: FREE home delivery of brand-new Love on Call novels, at least a month before they are available in the shops, FREE gifts and a monthly Newsletter packed with information.

Accepting these FREE books and gift places you under no obligation to buy, you may cancel at any time, even after receiving just your free shipment. Simply complete the coupon below and send it to:

MILLS & BOON READER SERVICE, FREEPOST, CROYDON, SURREY, CR9 3WZ.

No stamp needed

Yes, please send me 4 free Love on Call novels and a mystery gift. I understand that unless you hear from me, I will receive 4 superb new titles every month for just £1.99* each postage and packing free. I am under no obligation to purchase any books and I may cancel or suspend my subscription at any time, but the free books and gifts will be mine to keep in any case. (I am over 18 years of age)

2EP5D

Ms/Mrs/Miss/Mr _____

Address _____

_____

_____ Postcode _____

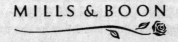